Nina's Irish Odyssey

by

William P. Sexton

PublishAmerica
Baltimore

First printing

This is a work of fiction. Names, characters, places, and incidents either are the product of the author's imagination or are used fictitiously. Any resemblance to actual persons, living or dead, events, or locales is entirely coincidental.

At the specific preference of the author, PublishAmerica allowed this work to remain exactly as the author intended, verbatim, without editorial input.

ISBN: 1-4241-8305-7
PUBLISHED BY PUBLISHAMERICA, LLLP
www.publishamerica.com
Baltimore

Printed in the United States of America

Dedicated to My Little Pals

Grandsons
Matthew & Ryan

Acknowledgement

My thanks to Margie Rafferty, who edited this book.
Despite her busy schedule,
she kept her word to help meet our deadlines.

Other Books by William P. Sexton (*aka* Liam O'Seasnain)

Liam O'Connor

I Have Not Forgotten Thee

Chapter 1

Moscow 1974

The Office of First Chief Directorate, responsible for all foreign activities ranging from intelligence gathering and espionage, to any form of bribery and assassination. Lt. Colonel Vladimir Zaitsev shook his head as he studied a photo of a twenty-year-old beautiful young woman. He tossed the photo over to Major Boris Kisliak, who sat opposite him. "Well," the colonel said, "have you ever seen anything as beautiful as that?"

The major laughed. "Yes, I have," pointing to a picture of his wife on the desk.

The colonel looked at him in disgust. "I was talking about a woman, not a cow."

This started the major laughing again; he reached over and pointed to the photo of the colonel's wife. "May I respectfully remind the colonel that many times, in his own words, he has admitted to having married an orangutan." The two men leaned back in their chairs and broke into belly laughs.

After a few minutes, Lt. Colonel Vladimir Zaitsev became very serious. "Let's get back to work. We have a covert operation to organize. This young woman was raised and trained for espionage work since she was removed from her mother, Contessa Garcia, at the Gulag camps twenty years ago. Her given name is Nina Garcia. Her mother was a Soviet agent during World War II. After the war, Contessa Garcia lived in East Germany. Contessa worked as a co-director of the communist youth party. The Director was Karl Gunter, her husband of many years.

"In World War II Karl Gunter was an officer with the Abwehr 1. His uncle was Field Marshal Gunter, who had his young nephew posted to Moscow as the German military attaché. The Field Marshal was always one of us. He believed that communism was the future of Germany. The Field Marshal's nephew was ruthless and a cold human being. It took very little persuasion to convince young Karl that communism was right for Germany. So while Karl served as a military attaché, he was secretly trained by the Communists to become a Soviet agent.

"While attending Russian classes at the University of Moscow, he met a beautiful girl who had joined the Communist Party. Contessa Garcia was a fiery young Spaniard, who was trained as a certified nurse with more guts and inner strength than Karl had ever encountered before. Karl soon seduced the young Spaniard. He recruited her for the NKVD, later to become known as the KGB.

"After attending the NKVD training camp, Contessa and Karl got married and left for Spain on their first assignment. Karl went as a military observer for the German Wehrmacht. Contessa was assigned to a Spanish army hospital in Madrid. There she met a wounded Martin Connolly, an Irish nationalist who had come over from Ireland to fight against the Communists. Karl Gunter and Martin Connolly became comrades in arms. Martin was wounded saving Karl's life in the village of Titulcia in Spain. The army hospital he was taken to was where Contessa was nursing. Karl had plans for the Irishman, so he ordered Contessa to seduce Martin.

"Many years later after World War II, she met Martin in East Germany with Karl, when they were directors of the Communist Youth Party. Martin had never forgotten her, and after attending the Leipzig fair in East Germany, he met her with Karl by accident in an old German restaurant, one they used to attend before the war. While at dinner he was shocked to find out she had been married to Karl Gunter all that time she had been professing her love for him.

"After they left the restaurant, Contessa came to Martin's hotel to try to explain to Martin how she set out to seduce him for Karl. In the process she had hopelessly fallen in love with him. Martin and Contessa were intimate in his hotel that night, which resulted in Contessa becoming pregnant. Martin never knew she was pregnant. They set a plan to escape. Karl became aware of the escape and had Contessa captured at the border.

"Karl had Contessa sent to a series of Gulag camps. Contessa managed to hide the pregnancy till the end. Contessa gave birth in Gulag Camp 109 to a little girl who was immediately taken from her. While Contessa was at 109, a sadistic commandant beat and damaged her back when he struck her with a rifle butt. A new commandant replaced the old one. He was a gentle and well-educated man and took pity on her, and he assigned her to a mobile unit where she went from camp to camp, always wondering about her love and the baby. She had only seen the child once."

The major shook his head. "Did she ever escape?"

"No," the colonel replied, "we have located her in Gulag Camp 8, near the Mongolian border."

"Does the girl know about her mother and father?"

The colonel looked straight out the window and then slowly turned towards the major. "We're about to tell her today. She will be here in about an hour's time. The party has enclosed an excellent report on her. She is quite intelligent and speaks Russian, Spanish, and English, and is proficient at kickboxing. Tall and beautiful, she seems to be without fear. The Party's report has pointed out she has an uncontrollable temper. They have given this some considerable thought, the conclusion being she may be able to carry out her assignments but must be watched carefully that she doesn't show signs of her temper interfering with her work."

The major sat wondering when the colonel would tell him of this woman's assignment. Why was he so preoccupied with his thoughts about this woman? Finally he remarked to the colonel, "Is there something different about this operation that would seem to be troubling you?"

The colonel again turned and looked out the window. "We've got to ask this woman to assassinate her father, to test her loyalty to us."

The major smiled and sarcastically said, "Since when does the KGB worry about asking our comrades to assassinate their relatives?"

Colonel Vladimir Zaitsev turned away from the window. "It takes years to train such a fine operative. If she cannot assassinate her father, she will defect. And then we will have an educated and trained enemy who knows us well."

The major asked, "Why would she assassinate her own father?"

The colonel replied, "I have here in my desk a bogus report to place in her folder. It states that when Contessa Garcia, her mother, tried to escape to meet Martin Connolly at the border, Connolly, filled with jealousy over her marriage to Gunter, had informed the border guards that she was escaping from her husband, Karl Gunter, who was a high official in the Communist Party. He also informed them she was carrying classified documents. When Nina comes here today, we will permit her access to her folder. After finding out the pain and suffering her mother went through, which eventually caused her death, this should activate that deadly temper of hers into killing Martin Connolly." The colonel handed over the report to the major of Nina's mother's capture and death, which the major placed carefully in Nina's folder.

***

Sometime later, one of the colonel's aides informed him that a young lady was waiting for him in the outer office. The two men stood up and straightened their uniforms and waited with anticipation for the door to open. When the door finally opened, in walked Nina.

The two men became spellbound. The young woman was exceptionally beautiful. Her dark raven hair hung low over her shoulders, her blue eyes penetrating them so that both men were forced to look away. She wore black tailored slacks with a black short-waist jacket, which was buttoned up to the neck. Black shoes raised her 5'8 height to about 5'10. One could see that she had dimples on both sides of her cheeks, but no smile appeared to show them off. She shook hands with both men, and the grip was both strong and firm, which took both men by surprise at the strength it possessed.

The colonel introduced the major to her and sat down. The colonel seemed lost for words and no help was coming from his visitor, who sat there staring at him. This colonel in the KGB was the man who had come up the ranks by murdering, torturing, and assassinating enemies of the state. To be captivated by a young woman like this was devastating to his ego. Yet he was not alone; looking across at the major, who seemed to be falling all over his words too, he had to smile. After some questioning about her training, the answers to which came short and to the point, he sat back and looked at her. She was starting to irritate him. Finally, with some tension in his voice he asked her, "You do realize you are here for an assignment?"

The reply was short. "Yes, Colonel, I do."

"I find your attitude and bearing to be a little arrogant."

"Well," she said, "if you and the good major would stop staring and get to the point, my attitude might change."

The colonel flew out of his chair, smashed the desk with his fist and shouted at her, "You little nothing, how dare you talk to me in that tone of voice. I could have you taken out and shot right now and no one would ever ask me why."

Standing straight up to him and practically in his face she shouted back, "I don't give a damn what you do to me. Shoot me! Go ahead, shoot me. I have given up worrying about dying since I was seven years of age."

The room was silent. The major kept looking at Nina, then at the colonel. It had been many years since anyone had talked to the colonel in this manner and that individual had been shot.

The colonel was taken back by the fiery young woman's words. He walked over to the window and after a few minutes, he picked up Nina's file and threw it at her. "Read it and come back when you have finished."

When she had left the room, the major went over to Zaitsev and put his hands on his shoulder. "What will you do with this one? There is no way you can let her get away with such disrespectful talk."

The colonel turned to him. "What would you suggest, Major?"

***

After reading the file, Nina returned to the colonel's office. She sat down and quickly pushed the file across the desk to Zaitsev. "Is my mother alive?" she asked.

"No," the colonel replied, "she died last year."

"How?" Nina asked.

"Contessa Garcia's strength gave out after years of beatings, bad food, and long hours in the fields finally took their toll." The major watched carefully to catch any reaction from the young woman. There was nothing in her facial expression that indicated sadness, concern or even pity. That ice-cold stare remained focused on the colonel. The major had been in service with different intelligence groups for nearly twenty years. Yet he couldn't ever remember anyone responding in such cool matter when hearing that kind of treatment of a member of one's family. The colonel sat back in his chair and tried to study Nina's face to see if he could read any kind of emotion.

Finally, Nina spoke. "What is my assignment, Colonel?"

"Major, could you please brief Nina in what is expected of her?"

The major, still fascinated by Nina's reaction, finally put his thoughts together. "We want you to assassinate Martin Connolly."

"Why?" Nina replied. "This man you want me to assassinate is my father. I can tell you within a heartbeat I will do it. But why now, after all these years, do you want him dead?"

The major looked across the desk at Zaitsev for his answer. "I'm sure you understand by now that any enemies of the state that have betrayed us are hunted down and eliminated, no matter what part of the world they hide in."

Nina shook her head. "This makes no sense. My father betrayed my mother, not the state. There must be other reasons for you wanting him assassinated."

"Nina," the colonel said, "your mother was a fine Soviet agent for years and she served the party well. She also was co-director of the Communist Youth Party. Karl Gunter was first reported by an informant to have betrayed your mother. It was said that Gunter had alerted the border guards when he saw her crossing over to the West, trying to escape with your father. Even when she was captured, Karl beat her in prison to give the impression he was punishing her for escaping, in hopes that the party would consider this to be punishment enough. Unfortunately, they felt otherwise. Despite Karl's hopes, he was ordered to send her to the Gulag camp. Karl Gunter died shortly afterward in a motorcycle accident. For years we consider Karl Gunter the original informer."

"Again, Colonel," Nina asked, "why did you wait so long?"

"Recently, one of the clerks was going over old records submitted by the border guards, which showed an entry of a telephone call made on the date your mother was captured. The entry read a call was made to the border guards about a woman who was attempting the cross over to the West carrying state secrets. A footnote indicated it was by a male with a distinct English accent. Later the operator who took the call identified it as being an Irish nationalist. Your father, Martin Connolly, was enraged at your mother's deception to him and he planned revenge on what he saw as a betrayal.

"Well," the colonel asked, "are you prepared to accept this assignment?"

The answer came swiftly. "Yes, my Colonel."

"Major Boris Kisliak will work closely with you." The colonel stood up. "Major, I leave Nina in your capable hands."

Nina and the major were about to leave the room when the colonel walked towards Nina and called her name. As she turned towards the colonel, he backhanded her across the face, knocking her to the floor. "My dear Nina," he said, "don't you ever talk to me in that way again or I will personally take you out and shoot you!" Nina, with help from the major, got to her feet. Looking into the colonel's eyes with hate, she left the room.

The major later told Colonel Vladimir Zaitsev he had felt her hate, standing next to her. The colonel laughed. "I promise you it will not detain me from my sleep tonight."

The major backed away and under his breath he said, "It would damn near worry me."

Chapter 2

Major Boris Kisliak introduced Nina to Captain Kriuitsky, who was second in command of Line F. This department was involved in kidnapping and assassination. The captain from the outset incorrectly evaluated Nina. He saw in her a future lover and he anticipated it would take a few months to seduce her while he was training her in the different ways to assassinate an adversary.

After a few months in the training course, he invited her to his office. Spreading out a map of West Berlin, he pointed out the hotel her father, Martin Connolly, was living and working in. Martin Connolly had remained in West Berlin for years after his beloved Contessa was captured. He hoped for some news or information that would help him find her. The captain pointed out routes of escape, should anything go wrong. West Germany was a hot spot for spies and the West German intelligence was operating under a high alert. So she was instructed to operate under strict precautions. Under no circumstances should she take unnecessary chances in eliminating her target. If the opportunity presented itself, then she was to proceed.

The captain sat back in his chair and took out a big cigar and lit it. Then he proceeded to study this potential assassin. He smiled at Nina. "This target, I believe, is your father. Will you not find this a very difficult task?"

Nina just stared at him. No sign of any emotion crossed her face. The captain got up from his chair and stood behind her, and bent down next to her ear and whispered, "You are very beautiful, and I believe deep down inside you are like all women, and emotion will get the best of you. This will lead you to failure. I will ask for a transfer for you to my office. There, you will have duties suitable for a lovely young lady like yourself." Nina remained silent and he took this to mean she agreed. He bent down and kissed her on her ear.

She sprang from her chair with the movements of a cat and as she faced him, she smiled. "I am meeting with Major Boris Kisliak in an hour. I will certainly send him your regards."

The captain sat in the dark for about an hour after Nina left. He was concerned what she would tell the major; she could damage his career. He had made up his mind not to have any romantic ideas about Nina.

Major Kisliak said good-bye to Nina at the airport and wished her luck. Still he noticed no emotion on her face as she boarded the airplane.

Martin Connolly lived at the Zimmer Hotel in West Berlin, where he worked as a concierge. Nina was to stay at this hotel and observe her father's working routine. The small hotel where he lived was easy to get in and out of. The residence was made up of an older clientele. Nina had checked in late in the evening and took a shower and immediately went to bed. The next morning, dressed in slacks and a warm woolen sweater, she went to breakfast. As she looked around the dining room, she could not find a table that the occupants didn't have gray or white hair. One old man winked at her, but she ignored him.

After breakfast, she went out to the concierge desk to find out about tours around the city. The concierge was in his early sixties. She found him quite humorous. After explaining what she would like to see in the different tours, he threw his head back and laughed. "Why in the name all that's holy would you be staying at an old folks' hotel like this? My good woman, who directed you to this hotel of the dead? They all have one foot in the grave, and that includes myself."

All at once she realized she was talking to her father. She was fascinated with his appearance; it was exactly like her notes. A man in his sixties, she thought he must have been quite handsome in his day, still with a full head of gray hair and eyes that seemed to show no age. She gave him a half-begrudging smile and told him she would like a personal guided escort around the city. She noticed that Martin Connolly was staring at her. At one point it seemed he was hypnotized with her. "Yes?" she said. "Is there something wrong?"

With a tear in his eye Martin Connolly replied, "No, no, Madame; you just remind me of someone long ago."

Nina asked him, "Was it someone you were close to?"

Martin Connolly looked down at the floor. "Close to?" he said. "She was the love of my life."

Nina could not resist probing. "Is she no longer with you?"

"No, she lives far away and we are separated by a high wall." Martin Connolly's remarks confused her. He must know he had her arrested. Yet he talked as if he loved her. What a hypocrite. The man who was her father captivated Nina. "Well, I'll tell you what I'll do, my darling. I will personally escort you after work to any place you wish to go."

Nina was confused with this man's dialect. "Why do you call me darling? I'm not your darling."

Martin smiled. "Ah, that's an old Irish expression, it means nothing. The Irish are devils for saying things like that." Once again she was confused. This man was talking about devils. Maybe he was senile. He said, "Tonight, my love, after six we'll go into town."

Now he's calling me his love. This man is ill.

20

That evening, Nina walked out of the elevator in a short black dress, high heels, and her raven hair down by her shoulders. Martin was waiting for her in the lobby dressed in his best suit. His heart sank as she approached him. "My God," he said out loud. "Oh Contessa, you have come back to me." Nina noticed that his hands were shaking, and she put her arm under his arm as they left the hotel. Suddenly Martin stopped and placed his hands across his face. He was sobbing. "Please excuse me," he whispered. "You see, I loved her so very much. I'm sorry I cannot go with you. I find that looking at you is tearing my insides apart." Martin turned and hastily left her standing outside the hotel.

Stunned and not sure of her thoughts, Nina went back to her room, where she spent the rest of the night in her chair, looking out at the lighted streets of Berlin.

Early that morning she was awakened by a knock on her door. When she opened it, she was surprised to see Major Boris Kisliak. "May I come in?" he asked. Still in her nightgown, she reluctantly invited him in. The major offered his apology for the early call and sat himself down in the chair that faced Nina. Nina sat on the bed and waited for an explanation. The major had trouble taking his eyes off Nina in her nightgown. Finally he told her that he was there to see if she needed some help with her assignment.

Nina looked at him. "This, I believe, is not the usual way the KGB babies their agents."

Turning red, the major told her he was there on another assignment and he thought he would look in on her. He also mentioned that as she was a new agent and this was her first assignment, he thought he might be of some help. Nina looked deep into the major's eyes. "Yes," she said sarcastically, "and of course it's because you feel fatherly towards me." This time the major turned beet red.

Nina ordered breakfast for two in her room. They found themselves talking for hours; Nina decided to tell him about her childhood. The major was aware of the contents of her file, but she now provided him with a description of her life with the Communists who raised her.

Nikolai and Natalia Kotov were members of the Communist Party. They were a middle-class family who lived outside of St. Petersburg. Nikolai was a ranking member of the Communist Party and his wife, Natalia, was a diehard Communist who would sell her own mother for the good of the party. Nina was entrusted to the Kotovs when she was a year old. They were ordered to raise her in the tradition of the Communist philosophy. Then, after university, she would be sent to the Illegal Directors for future training.

Nina told him how Nikolai beat her from the time she was six years of age. The beatings were nothing to compare with what his sadistic wife, Natalia, bestowed on her. Each day she would find a way to punish Nina for the smallest infraction of the rules. She would hold back her meals, and there were days that the little girl would go without eating one meal. She constantly beat Nina with a wooden cooking spoon, which left her black and blue all over.

Every year until she was seventeen, a member of the Communist Party would come for a report on Nina's progress. Nina would be given tests on the Communist doctrine. The major was listening very carefully as the young woman unfolded her tale. She continued to explain to the major that she was never allowed to date boys or have any friends; she grew up hard and with very little feelings. She recalled when she was seventeen years of age and Natalia came to her room to beat her for forgetting to bring in some groceries. Natalia began beating her with her fist; Nina put a stop to this by beating Natalia within an inch of her life. After she finished beating her, Nina kicked her down two flights of stairs and broke her arm. The party was informed and the investigation revealed the life Nina had with the Kotovs. Even the party couldn't put up with this situation. They knew this kind of anger could turn her away from the party; she might defect or even worse, become a double agent for a foreign intelligence.

The conversation for the remainder of the day finally got around to the major asking her how she was progressing on her current assignment. Nina walked to her window and, looking down at the Berlin Street, she seemed to be deep in thought. "I thought when I would meet him I would enjoy killing him to avenge my mother, but when he talks of my mother, I don't know, it's the way he looks when he mentions her—I must be very like my mother. I feel this man did love her, but it doesn't seem to add up to the report in my file. I will get him to take me on a tour tomorrow and I will find an opportunity to kill him." Shortly afterward Major Kisliak left the room.

The end of her stay was tomorrow; she was to return to Moscow immediately. Major Kisliak had left that morning. Waiting in the lobby to greet her was Martin Connolly. "My old heart is jumping with joy because I get to take you touring this morning. I promise not to act so melancholy. I will be nothing but pure joy to be with." She couldn't help thinking this man could charm Stalin himself.

All this was a façade for Martin Connolly, her father, who was in pain. He could only see Contessa in her and his heart was breaking just looking at her. If only she was staying there a little longer so he could see her, just once in a while. To him, Contessa had come back to him. Even to her movements it was Contessa. The only difference he could see was the color of her eyes. Contessa's eyes were a dark brown, and the only time

Martin had seen blue eyes like this was in Ireland. "I was wondering," he said to her while they were getting into the car, "is there any Irish blood in you at all?"

Nina smiled at him. "Not one drop."

Martin was taken back by the way she said it. "I take it you don't fancy the Irish too much."

"I heard they were a scruffy lot," she said.

Martin's face grew red. "Oh, it's because you don't know us. After one trip to Ireland, you'll be in love with the lot of us. Now let's get on our way. What would you like to see?"

"I would just like to ride around. I don't want to see anything in particular."

So for hours Martin rode around the main streets of Berlin. The conversation was sparse. Nina spoke very little to Martin. She was busy looking for the right spot to shoot him.

Finally, at a remote roadside, they stopped. While Martin was pointing out the scenery, Nina slipped the silencer pistol out of her coat and pointed the gun towards the back of Martin's head. Her arm started to shake and she had trouble in pulling the trigger. This was her father. She was starting to feel some form of connection to him, but she couldn't tell exactly what this feeling was about. She had never experienced this sort of emotion for anyone in her young life. She slowly removed the pistol from Martin's head and put it back in her coat. Martin was so preoccupied that he never noticed the gun.

The next day Nina left the hotel and was waiting for a cab to take her to the airport. As she opened the door to the cab, a strong hand grasped her arm. It was Martin, all dressed up in his Sunday best, and in his other hand was a bouquet of red roses. "God love you, I will miss you." He reached out to her and put his cheek next to hers. "I don't think you will ever know how much you have brought into my life, just being here." Nina turned from him and got into the cab. All the way to the airport she was wondering why she couldn't show one gesture of kindness to him.

Major Boris Kisliak was waiting for Nina at the airport in Moscow. "Welcome back, Nina," he said with his arms reaching out to her. Nina was tense. She knew by now Moscow was aware that Martin Connolly was alive and she had failed her first test of loyalty to the KGB.

Major Kisliak directed her to a table at one of the coffee shops in the airport. After ordering some strong Russian coffee, he looked directly into her eyes. "I have reported to Colonel Zaitsev that Martin Connolly is dead." Nina sat quietly sipping her coffee. Her thoughts were racing through her mind. Why had he done this? She waited for an answer but none was coming. "I've been instructed to house you at the Moscow Hotel in the center of Moscow. There will be no need for you to appear at headquarters anymore. I will be your controller. All your assignments will come directly by me. It is better that you are not seen at headquarters. The CIA have agents that watch the comings and goings of all personnel." After settling her in at the Moscow Hotel, Major Kisliak instructed Nina to rest for a few days. He would contact her shortly with her new assignment.

The following day Nina slept nearly twenty-four hours. She was emotionally exhausted. Martin Connolly had brought out feelings in her she never experienced before.

Nina was having a late dinner at the hotel when she looked up and there stood Major Kisliak. He sat down opposite her. "You're looking lovely tonight," he remarked. She continued eating and got a chuckle from him. "Nina," he said, "you never cease to amaze me. I have never met anyone like you before. We must talk. Let's go for a walk."

In the Moscow night air, Nina felt cold and the major offered her his overcoat. Major Kisliak was in civilian clothes. No thank-you came from Nina and once again the major smiled at her. "I received your new assignment. You are to leave for Nicaragua. I will be accompanying you on this assignment. After we land in Nicaragua we will be taken to a helicopter site, where we will meet with agents who operate in the jungles of Magar with the Sandinista guerillas. A plot to kidnap the American Ambassador to Nicaragua had been arranged by the Sandinista. They wanted the FSLN prisoners free, and a million dollars turned over to them. The American Ambassador escaped and we believe our agent involved in the operation warned the CIA. He was probably turned by the CIA and became a double agent. We want him assassinated and you have been picked to perform the assignment."

Nina was stunned. "Why me? This sounds like an assignment for an experienced agent."

"We are meeting with this agent late at night in the jungle. We believe he will not suspect a lone female approaching him. The element of surprise will be with you. We will pick up the necessary equipment you will need when our helicopter lands at the designated clearing. There we will be met by two army officers. These men have been leading raids with the Sandinista guerillas on the government National Guard patrols."

Chapter 3

June 1975

The helicopter landed in the midst of the Nicaraguan jungle. Upon landing, they were met by two undercover Russian officers attached to the Sandinista guerillas. The older officer reached out and shook hands with Boris and introduced the young officer to him. "I believe, sir, you are familiar with this gentleman, Ivan Kisliak." A huge smile came over the major's face and he reached over and embraced his son.

Turning to Nina, he said, "This is my aide, Nina." Both the officers seemed to be taken with her appearance.

That night while they sat around the campfire, the captain turned to the major. "I believe, sir, your son plans some form of entertainment for you." To the surprise of the captain and his guest, the young lieutenant appeared out of nowhere in ballet tights. His audience was in shock and Nina couldn't help but smile, not at Ivan but at the reaction of the captain and his Sandinista guerillas. It was a very humid night and Ivan danced to a fevered pitch. Fully exhausted and out of breath, he looked for some sign of pleasure from his father. The only emotion he could find in his father's face was deep shock and despair. Then, Ivan turned to his comrade in arms to find some kind of acknowledgment, he found only a stunned audience. Turning away, he disappeared into the jungle night.

That night the major sat away from the others. He was joined later by Nina, who sat down next to him. He started to rant and rave to Nina. "I am one who appreciates the ballet. I have seen many of the most famous ones. For a Russian officer to behave like this in front of the men is pure lunacy."

"I imagine he was trying to entertain you," Nina replied.

"Entertain me? He has shamed me in front of the Sandinista fighters. I should have never entered him into the Russian military. He was always a sensitive and a soft young man. The hard life of the military was a poor choice for me to have given him." Boris looked to Nina for some sign of compassion, but as usual, only a dead stare was across her face.

The following night they were attacked by a government National Guard patrol. The Sandinista guerillas beat them back and when the fighting was over, the captain took the major aside and said, "I have some disturbing news for you."

The major, in a show of alarm, asked, "Is my son dead?"

"I haven't seen him since the attack. I wish," the captain said, "this was the case. I must inform you that during the battle, your son deserted. He was seen heading deep into the bush. What are your orders, my Major?"

Without the slightest hesitation, Boris Kisliak told him, "Find him and bring him back."

"Sir, if I might suggest, we might report him as missing. As you well know, the penalty for desertion is death. If he's brought back, I'll be forced to shoot him."

Looking irritated at what the captain said, he shouted at him, "Bring him back! Bring him back!"

The following night, Nina met with the agent in the designated spot in the jungle. Nina arrived later than she should have. The agent, a Sandinista, had his back to her as she approached him. Her orders were to kill him. Without any reservation, Nina moved within an inch of him and placed her silencer pistol to the back of his head and fired. He fell forward onto the jungle floor. In training camp, the instructors were constantly amazed at her skill at approaching her target without being detected.

Nina bent over the agent's body, going through his clothes for any intelligence information he might have on him. Suddenly her head was pulled back and a knife blade was underneath her throat. Someone else was as proficient in sneaking up on their victims as she was. The voice was male and deep. He ordered her to drop her pistol. Standing her up quickly, he took the pistol from her hand and threw her up against a tree. With his knife pointing to her throat, he searched her roughly from head to toe. The hands were strong and firm.

"Before I kill you," the voice said, "how did you find out about the agent? I can make this quick or slow, it's up to you."

Nina looked directly into his face. Although it was covered with black make-up for the jungle night, his blue eyes were piercing and she managed to speak, although the knife remained under her chin. Nina's own piercing blue eyes looked into his and without any emotion, Nina told him, "Do your damnedest."

It was obvious he was taken back by her courage and lowered the knife. "Are you GRU or KGB?"

Without hesitation she told him she was sent by Moscow to kill this agent. "I wish to be a double agent for the CIA. I hate the Russians. They killed my mother and raised me in a Communist family to train me for the KGB."

"I'm with the CIA, but why the hell should I trust you?" he asked. "It's obvious that you're trying to save your life. Or do you really want to become a double agent?"

So swift was the knee that he didn't see it coming. Before he knew it, he was on his back with Nina sitting on him. It was his turn to have the knife pointed at his throat. The embarrassing part was that it was his own knife. She backhanded him across the face. "That was for being overly familiar with your hands while searching me." With that, she turned away the knife and stood up.

Slightly enraged and still simmering at her, he said, "You're quite a woman, aren't you?"

"Yes," Nina replied. "Too much woman for you, Yankee."

He threw back his head and started to laugh. "Let's talk."

That night they made arrangements to meet in Moscow. If he did not make it, one of his people would contact her.

Nina returned to the camp and reported to the major that she had completed her mission. Major Kisliak barely heard the report. She could easily see he was preoccupied; they had brought back his son and were prepared to execute him. "What will you do?" Nina asked him.

"I cannot have the captain execute him. It is my duty and my fault for the position he is in."

Cold and without any feelings whatsoever, she told him, "Do it."

Major Kisliak looked at her and he asked himself, *Does this woman have no soul?* Yet he was deeply attracted to her.

Later in the evening they both visited the major's son. He was held captive at the other end of the camp. When Ivan Kisliak saw his father, he threw his arms around him and started to cry. "Will they shoot me, Father?" he asked.

"Yes," the father said without any reservation. "You are a deserter."

"Father, surely you won't let them do this to me." Boris turned his head away from his son. Nina could see tears running down his face. The older man turned to leave and his son caught his arm. "I never wanted to join the military. I did it to please you. I love the finer things in life—music, opera and the ballet, good books. I've never been as strong as you, I knew this from the beginning and I never fooled myself into believing I could be like you. I don't want to die, please, Father," he begged, kneeling at his father's feet. The older man, clearly embarrassed by his son's behavior, quickly pulled away and left his son.

The next morning the captain, Nina and the major went directly to where Ivan was being held. Major Kisliak, with his pistol in his hand, came upon his son, who was lying on his side. Kneeling over him, he shook his son to awaken him, then he rolled his son over on his back. There was no need to shoot him; he was dead. After the examination, the captain found Ivan Kisliak had been shot to death.

Aboard the helicopter, the major pondered over who actually shot his son and why. Nina looked at Major Kisliak and asked, "Would you have actually shot your son?" Major Kisliak looked out the window of the helicopter and said nothing.

Chapter 4

Nina returned to the Moscow Hotel and Major Kisliak returned to his headquarters to report to Colonel Zaitsev. Three days had passed with no word from the major. Maybe something had gone wrong.

At about three o'clock in the afternoon on the fourth day, Nina received a letter slid under the door of her room. Anxiously she opened the letter. It was not from Major Kisliak, but from the CIA agent she met in the Nicaraguan jungle. The letter asked her to meet him at the Irish trade export board that evening.

When she arrived there, she found the export trade show in progress. Trying to seem interested in the Irish products, she anxiously awaited her contact. Nina always assumed that she was under the watchful eyes of the KGB. This was a normal procedure—to observe the comings and goings of their own agents. Nina held up one of the Irish sweaters to herself to measure for size when a voice with an Irish accent spoke to her over her shoulder. "I believe that's your color," the voice continued.

Nina turned to see a tall, sandy-haired man in a business suit smiling at her. That night in the Nicaraguan jungle, the face of the man she met had been covered in black soot. It would be hard to recognize him, but she would never forget those blue eyes that had focused on her that night. Somehow she thought his eyes were very much like her own.

The tall man whispered to her, "We must talk." Nina smiled at him as if he said something of humor to her. She whispered the name of her hotel and room number. "Tomorrow night at nine pm." The tall man moved away and disappeared into the crowd.

Nina tried the next day to occupy herself, but her thoughts kept going back to her meeting with the tall man in the jungle. Finally, that night at precisely nine pm, he arrived. This time he wore a black leather jacket and a black turtleneck jersey. She couldn't help but notice he was quite handsome. "We must be extremely cautious," he said. "It is very difficult operating here in their own ballpark."

Nina studied him for a few moments. "You're not American."

"That's right. I was born in Ireland, but I am a CIA officer. My name is Kevin Burke. We will accept for the time being that the reasons you are joining us are of a personal nature. At any rate, we're willing to take the chance that you wish to help us. Normally, we would have no trouble setting up a drop zone or a place to meet, but this is Moscow. Next week, we will meet by accident on a crowded street in Moscow. There I will give you an address to attend an Irish party that night, which will be attended by Irish businessmen. The Russians seem to like the Irish, so I believe they won't be as vigilant as to who will be attending the party. Although they haven't much faith in the Irish as would-be Communists, they believe that we are not willing to dedicate ourselves to that cause; this is true."

"What would you have me do?" Nina asked him.

"Well, tell me again why you are willing to betray your own country?"

A flash of temper crossed her face. "These people killed my mother."

"And what about your father?" he asked.

"He was an Irishman just like you. His name was Martin Connolly."

"Did you ever meet him?"

"Yes," she replied, "I was supposed to assassinate him."

Burke's reaction was one of shock. "Why?" he asked.

"They said he had betrayed my mother. Later I found out from a KGB contact that they had deceived me. My father and mother were trying to escape Karl Gunter, a German Communist, who was married to my mother at that time. He was the one who tipped off the border guards of her attempt to cross over into West Berlin."

"Have you ever seen your mother?" he asked.

"No," she replied.

"So what are you trying to tell me? When you were sent on this mission to assassinate your father, you thought he was responsible for betraying your mother." And then he asked, "Did you kill him?"

"No," Nina said.

"Why?" Burke answered.

"I just couldn't do it and I don't know why."

Burke threw his head back and started to laugh. "So you are not such a hard case after all."

Nina moved towards him and she said, "You're not too good at appraising people, are you? Because that double agent of yours wasn't lying in the jungle shot in the back of the head by a chimpanzee."

Burke couldn't take his eyes off her. She was absolutely stunning, standing there in front of him. She was wearing a tight, light blue blouse that emphasized her well-formed breasts and a black short skirt that was as tight-fitting as the blouse, showing that this lass was all woman.

Nina quickly reacted to his undressing her with his eyes. "Stop it! Stop it! You are no different from all the other male animals out there. Let's understand each other. I will work with your CIA but don't you ever put your hands on me. Do you understand?"

A smile crossed Burke's face. "I will be waiting for your call."

Nina shot back, "The Americans have an expression: Don't hold your breath."

"Aw, my love, as I told you, I am not an American. I'm a full-blooded Irishman and I can tell you now where I come from, no one, and I mean no one, ever gives up. It's not in our nature to surrender and before you and I are finished with our work, you will tell me that you love me."

Nina burst out laughing. "The Russians are right about what they say about the Irish. You are all dreamers! Now if you're finished with all this foolish talk, tell me what you expect of me. And keep in mind the kick in the nuts I gave you in the Nicaraguan jungle that night."

"How can I forget?" Burke replied. "It certainly made an impression on me. I would like a list of your contacts—who you report to and what your past assignments were. What is your next assignment? Is it possible that you can get someone higher up in the command to work with us? Someone who sets up the assignments for the center, knows names and where they are located. Most important to us is a list of any agents you know now who are working as moles in our security system."

Nina put up an open hand and said, "Wait a minute. I'm just a new recruit. I have no access to that kind of information."

Burke asked her, "What is the name of your controller?"

She replied, "Major Boris Kisliak."

"Yes, Nina," Burke replied. "I know him. The agency is well familiar with Major Kisliak. He is an assistant to Colonel Zaitsev of the Illegal Directorate."

Nina was surprised that he knew so much about the colonel's department. "I know," she said, "that Major Kisliak is attracted to me."

"Good," Burke remarked. "Win him over and you'll be able to help us more than you realize. This man and Colonel Zaitsev have access to all the information we are looking for. What is your next assignment?"

"I don't know yet," Nina told him.

Burke sat down on the edge of Nina's bed and gave her a list of places and drop-offs she must memorize, then destroy. "When you need to get in touch with me, there is a tobacco store in this hotel. There is an old lady who works behind the counter. She thinks she's working for the KGB, One of our agents a while back approached her as a KGB agent, soliciting her services for the state. This woman is our means of contact for our agents. After you're gone she will call a number and I will know that you'll be at the designated spot I have marked off for you, which you will have memorized."

Once again, he went over her drop-off's for placing messages, and promised to meet her in the local art gallery the following week. When he left the room, Nina felt a moment of loneliness. She quickly pulled down the covers of her bed and went directly to sleep.

There was no word from Major Kisliak and by the end of the week, she went to her meeting with Burke. Leaving the hotel, she made sure she was not being followed. Nina was in the gallery for nearly a half an hour and no sign of Burke, so she returned to the hotel. There in the lobby was Major Boris Kisliak and with him was Colonel Zaitsev. Nina tried to show no concern, but she couldn't help wondering why Colonel Zaitsev was there.

The two men led her into the hotel restaurant, where they proceeded to order lunch. Nina could not read any sign of emotion from either of the men. Finally Colonel Zaitsev smiled at her and said, "We are very pleased with your work, and Major Kisliak has been telling me good things about you." Nina's tension eased slightly as she waited for Colonel Zaitsev to continue. Speaking quietly, he told her he had another assignment for her—she was going to America, and Major Kisliak would brief her on the operation. They chatted for a while during lunch, but it was a conversation for those dining around them.

After Colonel Zaitsev left, Nina asked Major Kisliak why Colonel Zaitsev would come all the way from headquarters just to tell her of her assignment. Major Kisliak smiled at her. "No, my dear, you haven't reached the status of that importance for a man like Colonel Zaitsev to go out of his way to meet with you. He is here on another mission. We have discovered a CIA agent operating in this area, and the colonel's here to trap him."

Nina's face flushed. She hoped that Major Kisliak didn't notice. "Do you have him identified yet?" Nina asked.

"Yes," Major Kisliak replied, "we are closing in on him and we'll have him sometime tonight. He has turned one of our agents whom he had contacted earlier last year. We have persuaded this double agent to keep the meeting tonight with him. We would like to make an example of this CIA Agent to the European community. It always looks bad when we expose one of their agents to the world. Spying is always considered a dirty business and so every once in a while we expose one of their agents. It makes the Americans look bad."

Nina was trying to find out, without showing any interest in the agent, if it was Burke they were after. She decided it would be too risky to probe into the matter any further.

Afterwards, Major Kisliak went back to her room and explained her mission to her. "Tomorrow you will go to the following travel agent, who is just down the street from this hotel. There you'll be given tickets and brochures, etc., to the United States. Monday next you will be leaving with this travel group that will be touring the United States for one week. Their first stop will be at Dulles Airport in Washington. After landing, you will disappear from the tour. The touring guide has been already apprised of what you will be doing. The tour guide is one of our agents. The military attaché in our Russian embassy in Washington is a GRU intelligence officer named Sergio Kalugin. He is on the CIA payroll; they have gotten to him. Kalugin was having an affair with one of the CIA's paid prostitutes and she blackmailed him into turning traitor. We want you to eliminate Mr. Kalugin. There will be assistance given to you on this assignment by our people over there. When you leave the tour group, there will be a young lady who will take you to a safe house. Do not discuss this mission with her; she is only the escort to your safe house. Then you will meet one of our agents, whose name is Anatoh Grushko. He will instruct you on how you will assassinate Mr. Kalugin."

When Major Kisliak left, Nina waited for about an hour, and then went down to the gift shop in the hotel lobby. She had to warn Burke, even if it wasn't him they were after. Nina waited till two older women, who were browsing around, left. Nina approached the old lady and asked, "Do you have any Condore tobacco?" The old lady smiled and nodded her head in recognition. Nina returned to her room.

Hours passed and no word from Burke. Did he get the message? It was becoming dark and Major Kisliak said they were to trap him sometime that night. It was now nine pm and she found herself worrying. Passing by the mirror that was on the bureau, she thought, *Can this be me? I have never given a damn about anyone or anything. It is a strange feeling. This last year it seems to me some things do matter and I don't like it. I was once free of all these crippling emotions.*

There was a knock on the door and she ran to open it. For a moment she didn't recognize the caller. It was Burke, and he was dressed in a Russian army uniform. "My controller," Nina said, "has informed me they're setting a trap for a CIA agent tonight."

Burke took off his hat and sank into the chair. "What makes you think it's me they are after?" Nina explained her reason and Burke listened carefully. "It sounds like me they're after. I have an appointment tonight at ten pm with an agent. I will not keep it. I am grateful to you for the warning." Nina ignored him. Burke told her he will have to get out of Russia. Nina asked him if he will go back to the States. "Yes," he replied.

"Well, I'll probably see you there," she said. Nina explained her assignment to Burke. He was very interested in what she was saying.

After hearing of her plans concerning the travel arrangements, he told her, "We will meet again." Burke started for the door and stopped, then turned around and reaching for Nina, drew her near him. He kissed her gently on the lips and finding no reaction, he tried again. This time she placed her hand on the back of his neck and returned his kiss with such feeling that Burke realized at once he had never been kissed like that before. Nina melted his heart with that kiss. The night drifted by with the two lovers embraced in a moment of passion as only lovers do. Kevin Burke left the hotel before dawn the next morning.

Chapter 5

Nina sat patiently in Colonel Zaitsev's office while the colonel fiddled with some papers on his desk. Finally, Colonel Zaitsev sat back in his chair and studied Nina while he prepared to tell her of her assignment in the U.S.A. He broke his silence. "Nina, we are still sending you over to Washington, D.C. This new assignment is a very important one. The Kalugin mission has been cancelled. I personally don't think you are qualified for this new assignment. It calls for a highly skilled and experienced agent. However, Major Kisliak has great faith in your ability. So much so that when General Bitnov from the center was here a few months ago, Major Kisliak convinced him that you are the operative he was looking for. The Center has been plagued with failures in the United States. Many of our illegals have been turned and are now working for the CIA or the FBI. Heads are about to roll here in Moscow if they can't produce some results. The good general is worried about his job.

"Recently the head of the intelligence bureau of Czechoslovakia, the S+B had a top meeting with our chairman. He bragged about their agency, which in 1965 had a covert operative in the New York and Washington, D.C. areas that was quite successful. When the meeting was over, our chairman called for an immediate investigation of this statement given to him by this Czech intelligence officer. Two days later, a file was submitted to the chairman. The file was of such interest to him that he spent the whole night studying the

Czech operation. The next morning he called in General Bitnov. He ordered him to study the file and to meet with him the following day. The next day the general was ushered into the chairman's office. The chairman looked across his desk at Bitnov and wanted to know why our junior partners, the S+B, make fools of our KGB. We are failing miserably in the United States, despite all our technology support, funds and supposedly intelligence smarts and our junior partners are coming up with successes. It's apparent to me now that this group has supplied us with top intelligence on CIA operations and also on the third world countries."

Colonel Zaitsev continued, "In the middle 1970s, the Czechoslovak Bicycle team came over to Ireland to cycle again the Irish team. The day of the event, an Irishman named Sean Watson approached one of the Czech team managers and speaking in fair Czech said he wish to spy for Czechoslovakia. Watson had studied the language at a college in Belfast, Northern Ireland. A month later a Czechoslovakian businessman, who turned out to be a S+B agent, met with Watson in Belfast. He was impressed with Sean Watson and made arrangements to send him to Prague. There Sean was interviewed by the top S+B officers. They agreed to train him if he would go to America and apply to the CIA for a position. Sean told them of his wife, Margaret, who in her own right was a top businesswoman. The S+B agreed to interview her in Belfast. The S+B visualized the Irish couple spying for them because the Irish were always well liked and not so easily suspected. The S+B went to the KGB for assistance with this project but was discouraged by the KGB, who claimed they had worked with the Irish before and they were not good agents. Their commitment to Communism was not reliable, so the S+B took on the project themselves. Sean came back to Belfast enthusiastic about his new friends. Margaret was less enthusiastic about this bonding with the Czech S+B intelligence. Margaret was more concerned about the IRA, who had promised to kneecap Sean for a botched job he had done on a Protestant militant.

"The Watson's immigrated to the USA where they became American citizens. Sean Watson received his Masters at a well-known New York university. He applied to the CIA for a Czech translator position with the company. He was accepted and soon was promoted to a unit that was analyzing Czechoslovakian intelligence. Margaret Watson was also hired as a courier because of her position with an Irish Export Company. Margaret Watson had easy access to Europe. She could go back and forth without any suspicion as to why she was going into Communist areas. The Watson's were able to work effectively for their S+B masters."

Colonel Zaitsev got up off his chair and approached Nina, who was sitting down listening to his briefing. "I have tried to put you into the picture," the colonel said, "so that you will understand your assignment. The Watson's have been very successful in America. The problem is that Margaret Watson has been turned by the CIA. Sean Watson is not aware of this.

"Nina, I want you to eliminate Margaret Watson, but as discretely as possible. If you can get close to her as a friend, it is always easier to assassinate someone who doesn't suspect you. We don't want the S+B to connect us with this assassination. It will give me great pleasure to call this S+B intelligence officer into my office and inform him I had to clean up a messy situation his agency had got themselves into." He turned towards the window and shaking his head, he said, "To give them their due, the information they have passed on to us was of the highest quality."

The following week, Nina landed in Washington, D.C. and went directly to her hotel.

Chapter 6

The following morning, Nina received two phone calls in her room. The first was from the security at the Russian Chief of Station in Washington, D.C. He came right to the point and informed her she was to be in Ivan Pasov's office at noon the following day. Before Nina could answer, the phone went dead.

The second call was from Kevin Burke. He told her to meet him at Tyson's Corner, VA at twelve noon. She was surprised to hear from him. Afterwards she realized that Burke had tipped off immigration that she was due to land in Washington, D.C. shortly. After she landed, the CIA had followed her to her hotel. Nothing brilliant about that.

Nina left the hotel early to meet Burke at Tyson's Corner. She was about a half an hour early, so she decided to window-shop until noon came. There was Kevin Burke, neither one minute too early nor one minute late. The CIA trained their men never to be early for an appointment, never to bring attention to oneself by standing around waiting for someone.

"Good morning, my girl," Burke said to her with a heavy Irish accent.

"Stop calling me your girl. I'm not your anything!"

Burke stood back. "Ah," he said, "another bad morning."

"Let's eat," she replied, "I'm hungry. And save that stupid Irish talk for someone who can appreciate it. I do believe not many would appreciate this idle chatter."

"Listen, woman, I don't appreciate the way you're talking to me. It is very apparent that you are not acquainted with the Irish.

43

Be careful when you talk down to us or you will quickly find yourself looking up at us."

They sat opposite each other while they ate, neither saying very much. Burke broke the tension by telling her she was to come with him the day after tomorrow to the Irish Embassy. They were having a party for the new Irish ambassador to America. Still fuming, Burke looked at her. "What hole did you crawl out of? You're as miserable a person as I've ever met. I noticed, however, you were not that miserable when you hopped into bed with me."

Nina's eyes flared with fury at Burke. No one had ever talked like that to her. After she left the Kotovs, she had met all kinds of men, but they were always polite to her or bowing down to her. Colonel Zaitsev was the first man to have ever struck her since she had become an adult. Leaning over the table so none could hear her, she looked directly into Burke's eyes. She said to him, "You really annoy the shit out of me. Why do you go on and on with this useless talk? 'My girl,' 'my love,' my ass!" and she leaned back in her chair.

Burke was raging inside. "Listen you smartass. We have you by the short hair and you will do every damn thing that I tell you! When you handed over the names of the moles in our security, you signed your own death warrant, so shut up and eat."

Nina pushed the food away from her and got up from the table. "I will see you in a few days," and with that she left the restaurant. Burke was kicking his ass all the way back to headquarters. It was not the first time he blew an assignment with his Irish temper.

At noon the next day, Nina was sitting directly opposite Ivan Pasov. He was a man in his fifties with hard, focused eyes that never left her for a moment.

44

"It would seem that your assignment here is quite secret. Will you be staying long with us?"

Nina shrugged her shoulders. "I have no idea of the time sequence."

Ivan Pasov was annoyed at the tone in her voice and at Moscow for not informing him of her assignment. Ivan could hardly control his anger. She was right, but she was also very disrespectful to him and his position.

Later that evening Kevin Burke was standing in the lobby of the Hotel Madison waiting for Nina, who would be going to the Irish Embassy with him. The elevator opened and out came a very beautiful young woman. Nina was dressed in a sky-blue cocktail dress with matching shoes. This evening she was wearing her hair up; Burke immediately disliked her hair that way and made a very direct comment about liking her hair down around her shoulders. That was another big mistake. Nina took him by the arm and positioned him in a corner on the lobby floor. "If you don't like my hair this way, I have an answer to that. Yesterday morning I was listening to this American wife telling her husband off at the breakfast table. I believe the expression was, 'I don't give a rat's ass what you like.' I'm beginning to like the American way of life."

Burke went into such a frenzy he could hardly get the words out of his mouth. "I'll give you some advice: Don't, and I'll repeat, don't ever start thinking that the American women's way of handling their husbands is the smartest way. The chances are you will never get a husband with that attitude. The American women are too damn independent. That is why this country has so much divorce."

Nina looked at him and smiled. "I repeat, Mr. Burke: I don't give a rat's ass what you like. Are you now ready for us to proceed to the Irish Embassy?"

They drove to the Irish Embassy in silence. Burke was growling like a dog when he escorted her to the embassy.

The moment she entered the Irish Embassy she noticed the difference. The atmosphere was of a traditional Irish welcome and there were traditional Irish set dances going on around the floor. She was fascinated with this dance. There were some wild yells while the dance sets were going on and Burke looked over at her and said, "I see you can smile now and then. A couple of Irish set dances will loosen you up."

She reached over and spoke into his ear. "There is another American expression I like: Get lost!"

Burke was about to retaliate when a middle-aged couple came over to them. "My, my, what have we here? It's about time, Mr. Burke, that you got yourself a decent woman. My dear, Kevin never ceases to amaze me. He is forever bringing dogs to these parties. At last he has found himself a beautiful woman such as yourself."

Nina smiled at this engaging woman who spoke with an accent she was not familiar with. "I think," Nina said, "we are going to become fast friends." Turning to Burke she said, "Aren't you going to introduce me to this charming couple?"

"This, Nina, is Mr. and Mrs. Watson from Northern Ireland."

Nina's face turned pale. This was the woman she was sent to kill. Nina was studying Sean Watson as he made conversation with her. It was apparent that Margaret Watson was the one with the enchanting personality. Sean Watson was dull and uninteresting; she wondered how he got the reputation with the ladies that were listed in his file. Nina realized that the couple's attendance was unknown to Kevin Burke. Nina knew she needed to get Margaret alone in order to become friendly with her.

Burke got Nina out on the floor and the Watsons joined them on a half set. She was having the time of her life; something in the upbeat of the music made her feel alive. She expressed this to Burke. "Why not, woman? The Irish blood is all through your veins. By the way, where was your father born in Ireland?"

Nina thought for a moment. "The file on my father said that he was born in County Galway, Ireland."

"That is strange, because that is where I was born." Burke remembered she had told him her father's name was Martin Connolly. "My parents live only a few miles from the Connolly family. My grandma, Nan Burke, delivered all the Connolly babies. I remember one of their children was named Martin. That must be your father. She also delivered my father, Timmy Burke, who was Martin's best friend. How small the world is."

While Nina was talking with Burke, she noticed Margaret Watson crossing the floor on her way to the powder room. Nina thought this would probably be her last chance to talk to Margaret alone. She excused herself and entered the powder room. Margaret was sitting there alone, putting on her lipstick. "Hi," Nina said, sitting down next to Margaret. "Listen," she said, "I was sent by Moscow to give you instructions on a new assignment. This is a high level assignment and for your ears only." Margaret wrote down a business address and made arrangements with Nina to meet her at midnight.

After saying goodnight to Burke, she went straight to her room. She could not help thinking of the enjoyable evening she had had at the Irish Embassy. She had never laughed so much before. It was not her nature to laugh or even to smile. What was happening to her?

Nina opened her suitcase and produced a .38 special. She quickly attached a silencer to it and laid it on the bed. Nina slipped on her dark black slacks and a dark pullover, placing the pistol with the silencer down the back of her slacks. She put on a short tan suede jacket and left for Margaret Watson's office. It was only fifteen minutes from Nina's hotel so she decided to walk it.

It was a little after midnight when she reached Margaret Watson's office. There was one small light on Margaret's desk. Nina, trying the door, found it to be open. She was surprised to see Margaret sitting in her chair, because the desk light had blinded her when she stepped into the room. "I hope I didn't startle you," Margaret said.

"No, it's just that I didn't see you," Nina said.

"Well," Margaret said, "what is this assignment you bring me from Moscow?"

Nina moved slowly behind Margaret's chair, spreading a large map on Margaret's desk. She pointed to an area on the map. Margaret leaned forward from her chair to see where Nina was pointing. There was a small click and Margaret lay stretched across the desk. Nina moved along side her and removed the silencer from her pistol. She placed the gun back in her slacks; her silencer was placed in the pocket of her suede jacket. After turning out the desk light, she left the office.

As she walked back to the hotel, her mind was filled with questions. How easy it was, she thought, for her to kill Margaret Watson. She had no feelings about what she had just done. What kind of a human being had she become? How could she kill without any emotion? Ever since she met Kevin Burke and her father, she had changed. Nina found herself examining her actions. There seemed to be no remorse in what she was doing, yet for the first time she found herself questioning what she had done. Kevin Burke was maddening and frustrating; he was running her emotions up and down like an elevator. She felt a deep passion for him, yet there was something else behind the passion. Nina had known passion before, but this was different. There was a feeling so deep inside of her that it felt like pain. Nina never knew what love was about; she was falling in love with the Irishman.

***

Nina had just been in bed a few hours when a persistent knock on her door woke her from a deep slumber. Half-awake, Nina opened the door and found Ivan. He pushed his way in. "Get started packing. You are to be at the Dulles Airport in one hour. There you will find your ticket to Moscow. We received orders from Moscow this morning that you be on this flight. No reason was given."

While Nina was packing, her thoughts went to Burke. She would never see him again. There was no way to get in touch with him before her time of departure.

Chapter 7

A smiling Major Boris Kisliak met Nina at Moscow airport. "Well done," he said. Nina was surprised he knew what had happened in such a short time. "Colonel Zaitsev wishes to meet with you at his office tomorrow at 9 am."

Nina asked, "Will you be there?"

"No," the major replied. "I am on an assignment outside of Moscow for a week. I will see you when I return."

Lt. Nina Garcia sat in the outer office of Colonel Zaitsev in her brand new uniform while she waited for the colonel's secretary to escort her into his private office. After waiting patiently for about a half hour, the secretary signaled her to follow him. The colonel seemed to be concentrating on papers that were on his desk while Nina stood at attention. While she was standing there, it reminded her of their first meeting. Nina could almost feel the slap the colonel gave her across the face because she answered him in a very arrogant manner. Suddenly, the colonel rose up and smiled at her. "Nina, Nina, how well you look in uniform. Please sit down. In ten minutes or so, General Ostrousky will be presenting you with a medal for your outstanding performance in your last assignment." Colonel Zaitsev stood up and moved away from his desk towards Nina, who by now was sitting down. Bending over her, he touched her shoulder. He informed her that evening they would be dining at a very exclusive French restaurant in Moscow. There was something very personal in the colonel's touch and she felt very uncomfortable.

It wasn't very long when the office door opened and in came General Ostrousky. He was a giant of a man and Nina couldn't imagine another medal fitting on his uniform. After he pinned the medal on her, he shook hands with her and she was wondering if she could ever use her right hand again. Within minutes it was all over and the general was gone. Colonel Zaitsev stood smiling at her. He reminded her of a jackal waiting to devour its prey. What was he up to? This was not his normal behavior. He was too friendly and she was feeling very uneasy with him. "Well, my dear Nina, we are all pleased with the excellent way you are accomplishing your missions." Finally, he dismissed her and accompanied her to the door. This time his hand was placed on her back. Again she felt uncomfortable. "I will have my driver call for you with my car at 8 pm. Please be in civilian clothes. I will look forward to a very pleasant evening. We have much to talk about." Nina was hesitant to look directly at him. It might show her true feelings for this man.

The rest of the afternoon, Nina tried to keep herself busy. She had time to think about the changes in the colonel's behavior. There was no doubt that her womanly instinct was telling her the good colonel was about to hit on her. She had no fear of the man physically, but if she was to reject him, there would be very severe consequences for her. If only Major Kisliak was here, he would know how to handle this. He was not due back for another week.

All too soon, the dreaded 8 pm arrived. There in the lobby of the hotel was the driver in his dress uniform. "May I say that you are looking very beautiful tonight?" She had tried to appear not too glamorous. Nina slid into the back seat of the car. Almost obscured by the darkness, sat Colonel Zaitsev. "My, you look exquisite tonight." At that moment, he placed his hand on her leg. Nina was thinking he is not wasting any time. The colonel had no subtlety to his approach. He was treating her with no respect. The restaurant was one of the finest in Moscow. Why would he go through all this grandeur and act like a common soldier in his approach to her? Nina ignored his tasteless manners.

They arrived at the restaurant at 8:30 pm. Nina was captivated by the style and grace of the gentlemen escorting their ladies into the restaurant. She suddenly became aware of the driver as he stood by the opened car door. "Oh, I am sorry for keeping you waiting, I was caught up in the delightful goings-on." Then she noticed that the colonel was standing next to her. He was making an attempt to take hold of her arm.

They entered the restaurant and it was very crowded. The voices were loud all around her. She could hardly hear what the colonel was saying to her. Then she stopped and stood silently as she took in the most beautiful restaurant that she had ever been in before. Everywhere Nina looked, there were beautiful crystal chandeliers. The ceiling of the restaurant was one large mural depicting Napoleon's retreat from Moscow. The ceiling was alive with painted characters of many French soldiers struggling in the Russian snow. Nina noticed the strain and pain on the faces of Napoleon's soldiers. Horses in the snow, broken-down carts and dead French soldiers scattered all over intensified the mural. She was so mesmerized with everything around her that she hadn't noticed that the colonel was tugging at her arm. It seemed their table was ready. It crossed Nina's mind how quickly they were seated while there was such a long line waiting. How could this colonel afford such a night out? Nina was captivated by the cutlery on the table, which was enough to hold her attention for the evening. The cutlery was the finest silver she had ever seen. Nina knew this because as a woman she was curious about what were the better things in life, even though she had never personally experienced them. Her eyes moved across the table and focused on the beautiful handmade Irish linens, the finest at that time anywhere. The glasses were made of a very delicate crystal. Nina was so engrossed with her surroundings that she never noticed the colonel in his fine tuxedo. It was dark in the car and he was wearing an overcoat.

"My dear," the colonel said, "you seem to be lost in thought."

"Yes," Nina replied, "this is the most elegant place I have ever been in."

"Enjoy, my dear. There could be many more such places at your disposal." He hesitated. "But you must realize, this sort of luxury comes with a price."

Nina smiled at him and said to herself, *I can imagine what that price is.*

The waiters were all dressed in high white-collar jackets with dark trousers. She looked at the menu and it was all in French. The colonel smiled to himself and thought he might show her what a man of the world he was. "Do you understand French, my dear?" Nina looked at him and he smiled again. "Let me order for you." The colonel ordered the meal in French for both of them. She was more concerned about what he ordered. Nina's eyes moved down to the floor. It was made of a rich-looking wood that she was not familiar with. It shined so bright that she could almost imagine many Russian women on their hands and knees laboring for days to bring this floor to such a shine. All the while, Colonel Zaitsev was engaging her in small talk, which Nina heard none of.

The dinner was served and Nina seemed to enjoy it, even though she never knew what she had eaten that night. The colonel from time to time would ask her if she was enjoying a certain dish but would speak of the dish in its French name. This was driving Nina mad. She was hoping that he would identify the dish by its contents.

It was during the dessert that the colonel leaned over the table and whispered to her, "My dear, you are looking beautiful tonight." Nina was certainly not dressed for this occasion. She had no idea of how exclusive this restaurant was, so she had worn a simple light-blue dress that fell at her knees. She wore high-heel shoes that were dyed to match her dress. A single pearl choker was fitted tightly around her neck. It matched a single pearl bracelet around her slim wrist. Her raven hair was loosely spread across her neck. The color of her dress matched those beautiful Irish eyes, yet she had the look of her Spanish mother. To her surprise, the sound of enchanting music came across the room. Seconds after the music started, the colonel was standing by her side. "Please, my dear, may I have this dance?" Nina had no recourse but to accept. It was a waltz and Nina noted from the beginning it was going to be a tight squeeze. The minute he put his arms around her, Nina, who was 5'10" with heels, noticed how short the colonel was. *God*, she thought, *how I hate dancing with runts*. He wasn't a bad dancer yet she had her hands full trying to get out of the very obvious moves he was making on her on the dance floor. Nina and the colonel returned to the table and the colonel ordered two cognacs. He never bothered to ask Nina her preference in what would be considered an after-dinner drink. This annoyed her, but she proceeded to drink her cognac.

A bearded man approached their table. He was wearing a very elegant, expensive tuxedo. His dark black hair was streaked with grey and he looked to be in his late 50's. She took him to be Spanish. He focused his attention on the colonel and spoke in Russian with a heavy Spanish accent. Colonel Zaitsev stood up from the table and introduced Nina to this man. "Nina, this is Mr. Gomez from Nicaragua. He is a businessman who visits us once or twice a year. This is Nina Garcia." When she looked up at this man, their eyes met and a cold sweat came over her. He had a look of hate in his eyes for her. "I am aware of this lady. We met some time ago in the Nicaraguan jungle." Nina could not place him. After a few more comments to the colonel, he left.

Colonel Zaitsev looked across the table at Nina and said, "That gentleman that I introduced to you was the father of the Sandinista you killed in the jungle on your second assignment for us."

Nina replied, "I don't remember seeing him that night in the camp."

"Oh," the colonel said, "He was there."

After the cognac, the colonel took Nina back to the hotel. They had some small talk on the way back but she could see the way the colonel was behaving, he was no longer interested in her. His final words to her as she left the car, "Please be in my office tomorrow at 9 am."

The next morning, she sat very quietly in Colonel Zaitsev's office as he proceeded to explain her next assignment. "I am sending you back to Nicaragua to locate a Nazi war criminal that we have been after for years. This is a personal matter for me. His name is Otto Koch, a captain in the SS Einsatzgruppen. This SS unit was given the task of ethnic cleansing. They were a special group that followed the German Army after they invaded the country. They were trained to execute Communists, Jews, intellectual leaders, etc., that would prove a threat to the Germans. In 1941, the Germans invaded the Soviet Union. I am from a small town in the Ukraine. The SS

Einsatzgruppen followed the German Army into my home town and executed my grandparents. My grandfather was a low-level official of the Communist Party. My grandmother was shot because she was his wife. After the war, I looked to find this Otto Koch, but he escaped me. I know he was the one who actually pulled the trigger on them because one of the villagers saw the whole terrible scene. The villager made excellent notes regarding the description of this man and listed all his physical traits. Otto Koch is now living in Nicaragua with his granddaughter. Mr. Gomez, whom you met last night, has given me this information on Koch for certain other information I gave him."

Nina's first question was, "Does Mr. Gomez know you are sending me to Nicaragua?" "No," the colonel replied, "but it would behoove you not to have him see you in Nicaragua. He would have no hesitation in killing you."

"Oh," Nina replied, "that is a great comfort for me to hear that."

***

After a week of briefing on her new mission, Nina was ready to leave for Nicaragua. Meanwhile, Major Kisliak was back from his mission. They met one evening for dinner. Nina told the major what had transpired at her dinner with the colonel. It gave Major Kisliak a chuckle over Colonel Zaitsev's pass at Nina. "I suppose there is nothing like an old fool," he said. While he was saying this to her, he couldn't help feeling sympathy for one old fool to another. He was very much taken with Nina. "Be careful out there," he warned her. "If Mr. Gomez should find out that you are in Nicaragua, he will surely try to kill you. I remember that night in the jungle when they found his son's body. He became enraged and I would not like to be at the other end of his vengeance."

The next day Nina left Moscow on her way to Nicaragua. She had to change planes twice to make the proper connections. Nina landed in Nicaragua in the late evening and went straight to her hotel. She slept for ten hours. She got up the next morning, showered and dressed quickly. It was very warm and she wore a pair of shorts and a form-fitting white blouse. She had a small .22 pistol that she slipped into her shorts. She was told by Colonel Zaitsev to take a bus that ran to a small town 20 miles south of the capital. The colonel felt that she could mingle in the crowd and bring less attention to herself than driving a rental car about town. Nina had that Spanish look to her so she would mostly likely pass as a local.

The ride on the bus she would not forget too easily. From the beginning, the bus was suffocating: she could hardly breathe. There was no room to move anywhere. The seats were made to hold two people but they were holding three. Nina sat in the seat by the window but the seat beside her held two men. The seats in front and behind her were occupied in the same manner. She wasn't able to move her head back or lean forward. There were passengers hanging off the outside of the bus. It was a nightmare. At one time, the bus swerved out of control and they went down an embankment. Two of the passengers were hurt, and had to be sent to the hospital. It took every bit of her determination to get back on the bus. The bus started up and continued its journey as if nothing had happened. Nina, who spoke Spanish, her mother's tongue, found herself inquiring from the other passengers if these conditions were normal. She couldn't believe what she was hearing. This was an everyday occurrence and this bus had at least one accident a day. The appalling conditions were normal on this particular route.

After many hours of driving, she arrived in the town where Otto Koch was living. She could see why he would pick this isolated town. Nina looked in all directions and couldn't see one house or building for miles. Well, if old Otto was hiding out, this was the place to be, she smiled. Oh yes, the town of sweet nothings, she laughed out loud. Nina was instructed by Colonel Zaitsev that Otto Koch came every morning to take his little granddaughter to the school bus. Nina saw very little life in the town. This town was obviously a stop-off for the bus going in another direction. Nina walked towards the few stores that were on the main street. She passed the sign that indicated that this was the place where the school bus stopped. She continued until she went into one of the stores that had some life in it. The store had the appearance of a restaurant, yet it seemed to sell all types of farm equipment. She approached the individual that she assumed was the owner of the store. He was waiting on a young couple who were eating sandwiches. They were accompanied by their two small children. Nina stopped to admire the children and tell them how beautiful they were. "I take it, sir, that you are the owner of this establishment."

"Yes," he said, "what can I do for you?"

Nina replied, "Is there anywhere that I can sleep for a few nights? I see no places for accommodation."

"No, I am sorry," he replied. "We have no such places of public accommodation."

Nina was now getting concerned. *Where the hell am I going to stay?* she thought. She turned once again to the owner. "I only need a bed for a few nights. I will be leaving shortly after that."

The owner looked her and asked, "What is your business?"

Nina told him that she was meeting a friend of hers two days from now. She came early in hopes that she could rest awhile before she would continue to travel on with her friend. She obviously made a mistake getting off at this town to stay over. She never imagined that she would find a town with no accommodations. This caused the owner to smile. "This is an awfully small country. Most of us are poor people. You are not in the capital now. I will tell you what I can do. I have a storeroom in my basement and you may stay there if you wish." Nina jumped at the invitation, although she was concerned what it was like.

Nina found the storeroom to be exceptionally hot and stuffy with all kinds of bugs and insects which she had never set her eyes on before. She slept the first night with the towel the owner gave her over her head. The next morning she sat by the window of the restaurant. The bus stop was directly across the street. Nina had a clear view of the bus stop as she drank her coffee. The school bus arrived at 8 am and picked up a small group of children who were waiting for it. She didn't see Otto Koch or his granddaughter at first. The bus was about to leave when a large black car came speeding towards the bus. After stopping in front of the bus, a grey-haired man came out of the car and opened the back door. He reached into the back seat and a blond-haired girl about 6 years old came out. Nina had no doubt that was her man. She made a note that it appeared that Otto Koch drove himself. Nina could see no one else in the car. Nina immediately formed a plan to get to Otto Koch. Since there was no one else in the car, Nina would get into the back of the car while Otto Koch was making sure that his granddaughter was safely on the bus.

Nina stayed in the storeroom all night. She spent the night remembering things she had tried to forget, especially growing up. She remembered the time she was the same age as Otto Koch's granddaughter and the beatings she received from her foster parents. Nina never slept that night. The dawn came slowly and Nina walked to a little sink and washed her face. Watching the sun rise from a small window in the basement, she prepared for her day.

The restaurant was opened at 6 am. When she went in for her breakfast, Nina sat by the window looking at the bus stop. She ordered some coffee and buns. The coffee was like mud. It took her all she could do to get it down. A few people came in around 6:30 but that was all. Nina thought that this was probably the whole town. To her surprise, it became noisy and loud. Nina couldn't imagine any noise or loudness in that restaurant from those few people. But it happened that way.

The time dragged by for Nina until the bus arrived. Shortly after, the big black car arrived. Nina waited for Koch to leave his car with his granddaughter. She was out of the restaurant in seconds and heading for Koch's car. She slid into the back seat and crouched down behind the driver's seat. Otto Koch returned to his car and drove away, not realizing that Nina was on the floor behind him. Nina let Koch drive for a few miles when she rose from the floor and placed the .22 pistol in the back of his neck. The sudden action unnerved Koch and he swerved back and forth on the road. Nina spoke calmly to him, which led him to straighten out the car. "What do you want of me?" he gasped. "I know you are Mossad. It took you long enough to find me." Nina smiled. "Not Mossad. Your friends from the Ukraine asked me to look you up." Stunned by Nina's last remark, Koch tried to remember. Nina ordered him to stop the car. "Get out," she ordered him. Otto Koch, the one-time assassin of women and children, seemed to be nothing more than an old feeble man shaking with fright and to Nina, not much of a man.

"Please," he said, "don't kill me. I have so much to live for. I have a beautiful little granddaughter who gives me so much pleasure."

Nina looked at him. "Yes, I believe you, but I can't help wondering how much pleasure you have given the survivors of those families you murdered. I understood you enjoyed your work."

Koch fell on his knees and holding his hands to his face, he asked, "Who told you such lies? I was never with the Einsatzgruppen Group."

Nina stood back from him. "I never mentioned the Einsatzgruppen Group." With that she shot Koch in the face. She rolled him over and shot him two more times in the back of the head. This was the professional way of doing it. Nina was sorry she had shot him in the face. She had lost her temper and reacted like an amateur.

Nina drove Koch's car about a mile out of town, where she got out and walked back to the restaurant. Nina sat down and had a cup of tea. She wasn't brave enough to have the restaurant's coffee again. Nina had tossed Koch's body in a ditch and she calculated it would be awhile before Koch's body was discovered. By then, she would be long gone.

The early bus back to the capital was about 2 hours late. This gave Nina some concern. She had figured she would be already on her way. The best of plans can go wrong. The bus eventually came and Nina was back on that wild ride back to the capital. How this bus got there she would never know. What an old rattle trap. Finally she made a connection to the airport. When she arrived there, she went directly to the bar, where she had three stiff drinks to bring back her heartbeat from that bus ride from hell. While she was sitting at the bar, her heart skipped a beat. "Oh no," she said out loud. There, standing directly behind her, was Mr. Gomez. He was looking at her in the bar's mirror. When he met Nina's eyes, he said nothing. Just smiled at her and moved away.

It seemed forever for the plane to load up. After a little while the doors closed and the engines started up. Nina started to breathe a sigh of relief as the plane taxied off. A call from the pilot over the intercom to the passengers indicated the plane was returning to the gate. There seemed to be some problem with the plane. Nina knew it was her that they were after. She started to plan a cover story. When the plane was at the gate, the doors were opened and two armed guards, one man in civilian clothes and the other in uniform, boarded the plane. They came directly to Nina's seat and escorted her off the plane. Nina said nothing because she knew it was useless.

When she entered the terminal, she was taken into an office where she waited for about an hour. Looking out of the office window, Nina observed the terminal. It was full of guards. The door suddenly opened and there he was, Mr. Gomez, standing pretty cocky and sure of himself. She noticed immediately the armed guards and two men in civilian suits, who were hanging on every word he said. This was an important man and they were showing their respect to him.

Mr. Gomez spoke and Nina was roughly taken by her arms out of the office. Nina was pushed and shoved through the airport. When they finally arrived at the end of the terminal, she was shoved into a waiting car. When Nina raised herself up in the back seat, she noticed the driver was a brute of a man. Sitting next to him was still a more sinister-looking character. It took Nina awhile to get her bearings when she became aware of someone sitting next to her. She looked quickly alongside of her. She needed not to take a second look. It was Mr. Gomez.

They rode for a long time till they came to a small cabin off the road. Nina could see that there was no sign of life for miles around. It was plain to Nina she wasn't coming back. Her captives showed no concern about her recognizing the area.

She wore no blindfold and the men in the car couldn't care less what landmarks she was observing.

When they entered the cabin, two of the men threw her on the floor in a small room. She heard nothing until the following morning. Nina was standing against the side of the wall in the room when the door opened and in walked Mr. Gomez with his two goons. Mr. Gomez moved towards her and she saw in his eyes a hate that gave her the chills. Mr. Gomez hit her with a closed fist that was followed by a long stream of cursing. Nina fell to the floor from the blow. Her head was spinning. She tried to raise herself from the ground and felt a sharp pain in her ribs. Mr. Gomez had kicked her as she rose from the floor. Mr. Gomez reached down and pulled her up from the ground by her long hair and kneed her in the groin. After standing over her, he said, "You have killed my son and I promise you that you will pray to die by the time I am finished with you." Mr. Gomez and the two other men left the room, leaving Nina on the floor in her own blood.

Nina was finally able to sit up with her back against the wall. She couldn't see her face but she knew it was all swollen. Blood just kept coming out of her mouth and nose. The pain from her rib cage was so intense that she couldn't take a breath. She assumed she had some broken ribs. Nina had no doubt that this was only the beginning. Mr. Gomez would surely kill her.

The next morning Mr. Gomez and his goons entered the room but in a less noisy manner. It was as if they were sizing up the situation. Mr. Gomez walked over to Nina, who was once again standing against the wall. He reached over and caught hold of her cheek and twisting it, he said, "You don't look too good this morning, my beauty." He looked at his two companions and laughed. That was enough for the fiery Spanish-Irish girl and she let loose with a closed karate fist to

Mr. Gomez's face, knocking him down. The other two men attacked at once. The first man received a karate kick to the groin and the other, a series of karate punches all over his body. Nina was heading for the door when she stopped short. There in front of her was a tall man with a pistol in his hand. He pointed the pistol at Mr. Gomez and shot him in the forehead and as quickly, fired two more shots, killing the other two men. Nina was standing there looking in amazement. "Who are you?" she asked. The tall man turned and walked out of the door. Nina followed him, asking once again, "Who are you?"

The tall man turned briefly and spoke, "I am Mossad!" He walked to his car and got in. All that could be seen was the back of his car heading down the road. Nina sunk to the ground and tried to get her composure.

Somehow, she managed to get into Gomez's car and drive herself to the airport.

***

Nina arrived in Moscow a few days later. She went directly to Colonel Zaitsev's office. When the colonel arrived at his office that morning, Nina was already there. The colonel took one look at Nina and shook his head. "There is no need to tell me what you went through. I can see it all. I am giving you a few weeks leave. Thank you for the personal service you have afforded me and I will not forget you."

Nina told the colonel about the tall man that was from Mossad. She wanted to know what that was all about. The colonel leaned back in his chair and said the Mossad had been looking for Otto Koch for years. "They were following him to see if he would lead them to more war criminals. But you got there ahead of them. So they had to act."

Chapter 8

When she left Colonel Zaitsev, she headed to the café that was directly across the street from Colonel Zaitsev's office. She had arranged to meet Major Kisliak there. After going over what had occurred in Nicaragua with Major Kisliak, she stopped abruptly and put her head down on her hands. She stayed that way for a few seconds and then she lifted her head up from her hands, looking directly in Major Kisliak's eyes. She blurted out, "I want to see my mother's grave."

Major Kisliak was taken aback. "I would say that is impossible."

Nina clasped her two hands together. "Please, Major, I must see her grave. I remember the file I was left to read at Colonel Zaitsev's office. That file indicated that my mother died in a Gulag camp."

Major Kisliak looked at her and said he would try to find out the Gulag camp her mother was last interned. Kisliak knew from Colonel Zaitsev that the report on Contessa Garcia said that she was still alive in Gulag camp 8 near the Mongolian border. Colonel Zaitsev would have to give his permission for Nina to visit the camp; this he would never approve. Kisliak would have to do this on his own.

Major Boris Kisliak sat patiently at his desk, facing Colonel Zaitsev. He had asked permission to take Nina to the Mongolian border. He told the colonel that Nina had always wanted to see the Mongolian country and as a reward for an outstanding job for the center, he would like to grant her wishes. The colonel hesitated for a moment and turned his chair to the window, which faced out on the city of Moscow. Major Kisliak waited patiently for his answer. Finally the colonel spun around in his chair and after a while, looking down on his desk, he murmured, "Fine. Get the necessary papers in order and I will sign them."

That evening at dinner he told the beaming Nina that the colonel had approved the trip and they would be ready to leave in two days. Nina leaned over the table and kissed the red-faced major on the cheek.

Chapter 9

Major Kisliak and Nina left the train that had taken them from Moscow to a small town near the Mongolian border. They traveled by private car to Gulag 8. The papers Major Kisliak had on him indicated he was on official business and were signed by Colonel Zaitsev. The way these orders were written could be interpreted to mean an inspection of the Gulag camp, which was exactly what Kisliak wanted.

The commandant stood up from his desk and seemed surprised at Major Kisliak standing before him with Nina by his side. "I have orders to inspect this camp," Kisliak said which left no doubt in the commandant's mind. He was dealing with authority. "I have not received any confirmation of your arrival, Major Kisliak." He was dismissed with a wave of Kisliak's hand. "These are my orders," presenting them to the commandant, then turning to Nina, "and this is my assistant. She will take the necessary notes. We will proceed immediately," the major said. "The center is not overjoyed with your performance in GUG 8 Camp." The commandant was about to speak when Kisliak looked straight into his eyes, "Let's get on with it."

After checking the different housing units that were used to confine the prisoners, they proceeded to the hospital. When they entered a room filled with rows of beds, they noticed only one nurse caring for the entire room. Major Kisliak called out to her to come over to where he was standing with Nina. The woman appeared to be in her late fifties or even into her sixties. The nurse approached them and it was apparent she had a back injury. Her posture was bent over and she was too young to be so stooped. "Yes," she asked, "what can I do for you?" The two women stared at each other. It was as if they had known each other.

Nina noticed immediately that the woman's hair was streaked with gray. It was full and vibrant. Nina thought it was the hair of a younger woman on an old face. The woman's eyes seemed to be searching for some sign in Nina's face that would indicate they had met before. Major Kisliak said nothing. He was waiting for something, anything that would break the spell between the two women.

The nurse touched Nina on the arm and directed her to the beds of the patients. Nina felt a strange feeling come over her. It was a touch she had felt before. The woman seemed to be trying to get close to her. Nina desperately wanted to put her arms around her but she couldn't understand why she felt that way. Kisliak could see Nina was emotionally moved by this woman. It was obvious to him she also was trying to make a physical connection. The nurse was losing her concentration from time to time. She seemed to fall into a trance staring at Nina.

The commandant appeared in the doorway and ordered the nurse back to her duties. Kisliak believed it was time to go to. To linger any longer might arouse the commandant's suspicions. Kisliak and Nina left the hospital, but not before Kisliak gave the commandant a good chewing out on the way he ran the camp. They were heading for their car when the nurse ran towards them. She spoke quietly with a strong Spanish accent that was not apparent to them in the hospital. She appeared out of breath and in pain from such a short run.

Placing both hands on both sides of Nina's face, she pulled Nina to her level and kissed her tenderly on the forehead and turned to walk away.

On the way to the train, Kisliak tried to explain to Nina that there was no evidence of her mother's grave. The Commandant had indicated to him that he knew nothing about Contessa Garcia's death. This was a lie but Kisliak couldn't reveal the truth to Nina, at least not yet.

When they got on the train to Moscow, Nina was silent for the length of the trip. Finally as they entered Moscow Station, she turned to Kisliak and asked, "That was my mother wasn't it?"

"Yes," he told her. He couldn't continue with the lies.

"She knew me. I felt it right to the dept of my soul."

The days grew long for Nina. Her thoughts were reaching out to Kevin Burke. Where was he? The chances were he wasn't giving her a second thought. She remembered the softness of his kiss. There were times she could still feel his strong arms around her.

Nina was back in Moscow for months and no attempt was made by the CIA to contact her. Maybe they had decided she wasn't worth pursuing any further. During the week, she lunched with Major Kisliak and she asked him for an assignment in the USA. If not, perhaps somewhere in Europe. Major Kisliak informed Nina that there was something brewing in Colonel Zaitsev's office, but it was all hush-hush.

Nina started running on a local Moscow track to keep in shape. She had been aware that someone was keeping pace behind her, but she was unable to identify who it was.

One day while running on the track, she dropped back and waited for the runner behind her. A young woman of about 25 came speeding around the bend. Nina jumped out at the young woman and demanded she explain why she was following her. "Nobody is following you," the young woman shouted back and kept on running.

Nina sat on one of the benches that were strung along the tracks. She found herself all tied up inside with these new emotions. In this business, one must keep cool. It was normal procedure to keep their new agents under surveillance. Nina returned to the hotel after finishing the last lap of the track and took a shower. The hotel rooms faced the Moscow streets. Nina opened the window and leaned out. In a small, compact car, she saw a man with his car window opened. He was looking up at her room. Who was he? CIA or KBG?

Late that evening, she had dinner with Major Kisliak. During the dinner, Kisliak noticed Nina was tense and appeared on edge. So, he put forth his observation to her. Nina sat back in her chair and placed a cigarette in her mouth and lit it. Drawing deeply from it and with some force, she exhaled. Leaning forward on the table, she focused her eyes on Major Kisliak, "I want my mother out of that Gulag camp."

Major Kisliak pushed away from the table and gave her a very concerned look. "If you try to get your mother out, Colonel Zaitsev will know I took you to the camp and I will end up there myself."

Nina's eyes were flashing. "If Colonel Zaitsev doesn't get my mother released then I will leave his department."

This brought a strong reaction from Kisliak. "The good colonel will kill you. No one leaves his organization until they are released by him. Please don't be a fool. Nina, you are experiencing the stress of this covert activity. It happens time after time with our agents. All but a few get over it. Those who don't, get eliminated."

"Major Kisliak, are you telling me that our own people are eliminated if they can't continue? What kind of a government did I pledge my loyalty to?"

"Nina, you are making too much out of this." Then the major told her he would see that she received no further assignments for awhile. "Nina, have you ever been to Ireland? After all, you are half Irish. It is one of the most relaxing places to have a holiday in. I have been there, years ago on an assignment. The people are very humorous and friendly. Maybe you could see where your father came from."

"My father is doing fine. He is not the one who is in the Gulag camp."

"Nina, you take the time out and go to Ireland. Then we will see what I can do for your mother. Leave that to me," he replied. Even as he spoke, he knew there would be no release for her mother. "Buy yourself some sweaters. Ireland can be damp even in the fine weather."

Nina departed from the restaurant feeling some hope that Major Kisliak would somehow get her mother released from the Gulag camp. After all, he had been able to arrange for her to see her mother.

Major Boris Kisliak was playing a very dangerous game with his colonel. If anything went wrong, it would surely cost him his life. KGB had a few trusted agents in Ireland and Kisliak suggested to Zaitsev that Nina could serve as a courier to two of the agents who had been complaining about not having enough money to operate in Ireland, and the usual way of getting it to them was becoming dangerous. This assignment would round out Nina's covert experience. The Colonel studied Kisliak's suggestion and after a little while, he spoke. "It would seem to me you are putting the cart before the horse. This agent so far has eliminated two of our enemies. Nina has proved herself to be an exceptional woman. Now you wish to send her as a common courier. What are you thinking, Kisliak?"

"Well," Kisliak replied, "we are in the process of establishing a new cell operation in Ireland. I believe that Nina would work out quite well. This trip will familiarize her with the country. It has been a good practice in the past to send out an agent without knowledge of his true assignment."

"Yes, I see what you are getting at. Major, make your arrangements."

When Kisliak left Zaitsev's office, he felt cold sweat on his brow.

***

Nina landed in Dublin, Ireland with 20,000 Irish pounds. It was concealed in her luggage. The customs were not overly vigilant that day. During the inspection, one of the customs men drew a smile from her when he laughingly told her to stay out of Cork. "They are an odd lot. They think there is no other county in Ireland but themselves. One look at you and they will claim you for their own." Nina went away trying to figure out what the hell he was talking about. Anyway, she got the money through. There were no restrictions at that time on how much money you could bring into Ireland. If, however, customs had discovered that large amount in cash it would have raised suspicions as to what she was doing.

The Dublin taxi driver had her laughing all the way to her hotel in the city center. It was a small hotel, and the receptionist at the desk was very friendly towards her. She was fascinated to see her in her exotic clothes from Russia. The room was small but clean and the view of the city was lovely. She noted that one could almost touch the clouds in Ireland. Everywhere she looked there was green, even though she was in the city of Dublin. After putting away her clothes and emptying her luggage, she placed it in the closet. She felt at ease. The 20,000 Irish pounds were hidden in the lining of her suitcase. It was as safe as possible for the time being.

It was a bright day when she walked up Grafton Street to explore the Irish department stores, restaurants, and specialty shops along the way. She walked into a coffee shop where she found a cozy atmosphere of jolly people. They seemed to be on their lunch hour. It also seemed to contain a fair amount of leisure shoppers by the looks of their shopping bags.

The little coffee shop was self-serving and there was a long line of customers, removing the goodies from the counters. Nina had never seen what they called bangers (an Irish sausage). An old lady standing behind her noticed her trying to make up her mind. "Ah love," she said with her Dublin accent, "try them and a few rashers (Irish bacon). It will give you a taste of old Ireland." When the old lady had finished filling her tray, she could hardly carry it.

The place was so crowded there was not a place to sit. An old gentleman got up from his table and gave her his seat. She ate every thing on the plate. It was delicious. It was all new to her. Nina was enchanted with the Irish.

Nina walked to the beginning of Grafton Street and saw a beautiful green park called St. Stephen's Green. The park on this summer day was filled with people just laying out on the green taking in the sun. It had a beautiful pond in the middle of the park, with ducks and birds all around it. After walking through the park, she made note that it was an excellent place to meet her agents.

It seemed to her that it must be lunch hour because most people in the park at that time were eating their lunch. She noted the time. She would meet her contacts at that lunch hour time. It would be a good cover among all these people. She walked over to the pond where the ducks were and watched the young couples feeding them. She was suddenly struck by the fact that there seemed to be so many young people around her, and that there were very few older people in the park. Also, Nina realized that she appeared to be much older and more mature than the girls who, she calculated, were around her age.

Nina walked along the park. Finally, she decided to lie down in the grass. She stretched out on her back with her face in the sun. Nina felt so at ease that she fell asleep with that old Irish sky above her. She was awakened by a soft kiss on her mouth. Nina was not able to identify the intruder because the sun was blinding her. She shot up in alarm and was met by two strong arms, which pinned her down in the grass. It didn't take long for Nina to realize that it was her crazy Irishman.

"Good morning to you," he said with a grin that would have swallowed a cow.

"My God," Nina said, looking around her to see who might have seen what had happened. That would have accounted for all of St. Stephen's Green.

"Go away with yourself," Burke said. "This is Ireland. The fellows over here are very romantic. Sure, we kiss anyone that gets in range." Nina couldn't help but notice that when he smiled at her, something inside her told her that everything with the world was all right. Once again, he bent over and kissed her gently on the lips. This time, she returned his kiss and at that moment the KGB and CIA could all go to hell.

They sat in the grass long into the evening lost in girl and boy talk. Nina found herself laughing at this Irishman. This was something Nina rarely did. The Irishman told one story after the other. Nina was thoroughly confused by the stories. She never could tell when he was making fun of her.

When the time came to go, Nina put her arms around Burke's neck and whispered in his ear. "I don't want to go. I wish we could go on like this forever."

74

Burke drew her arms away from his neck and looked deeply into her eyes. "This lot that you have chosen to be involved with is very dangerous. They would never let you walk away from them. I have not informed my people of our relationship. They only know that you have handed over to me some names of moles operating in the CIA and FBI."

"Oh please," Nina said, "tell me you are squeaky clean and that the CIA would not shoot one of their operatives." She started to laugh but it was a nervous laugh and became non-existing when she noted that Burke was not laughing.

Nina walked along the park with Burke. She was in a playful mood. Burke tried to get her in a serious mood and was becoming frustrated. Suddenly, she stopped, "Oh it was fine when you were all full of funning but now I must calm down and act like the professional that I am suppose to be. Listen my Irish friend; there is a saying in the lobby of my hotel, 'What is sauce for the goose is sauce for the gander.'" She reached up and kissed him.

Kevin Burke knew he had found himself one hell of a woman.

The next few days, they rented a car and Burke took her down to Galway to see his home. His mother was still alive and living in the old homestead in Connemara, Co. Galway. The old woman threw her arms around her handsome son and Burke spun her around the room. Nina watched and thought to herself, what she would have given to have her mother in that room at that moment.

The old woman's eyes fell on Nina. She looked at her up and down until Nina became uncomfortable. Then she went over to her and hugged her. "I don't know where you are from but I know somehow there is Irish blood in you. She looked back at Kevin and said, "Oh, she is a fine broth of a girl you have there."

Burke started laugh. "Right you are mother, but she needs some training."

Nina reached up and caught Burke by the nose. "Try it," she said. The old woman laughed.

"I have just made some brown bread and we'll have a cup of tea, won't we?" she said. The Irish have a tendency of asking a question when they are making a statement.

Kevin Burke's mother was a big hit with Nina. She loved her brown bread. They sat down in front of the old fireplace, which had been there since the house was built. It was one of few houses that still used the turf from the fields to heat the house. The three sat all night talking about the Burke family. Finally, they got around to sorting out the relationship of Nina's father to the Burkes. Nina's father Martin Connelly was well known to the Burkes. Nina listened with great interest as the old woman told stories about her father.

When Nina finally went to bed, which was nearly morning, she lay quietly in the bed going over all the stories of her Irish relatives. The faces of her father and mother were now before her. She started to fill in their characteristics and personalities although she had still very little knowledge of her mother's family or even facts about her mother herself. She marveled at the courage and strength of her mother in surviving in that Gulag Camp.

Chapter 10

The following morning, Burke took Nina for a ride to her father's house. Nina came to a hill that looked down on her father's house. It was the same place her father stood when he left for Spain in 1936 to fight for his faith. That was when he was wounded and sent to the Spanish hospital where he met Nina's mother and fell in love with her. A love that would last for a lifetime. In 1969, Martin Connolly returned to Ireland. He stayed for a short time and returned to Germany to await the return of Contessa, now in a Gulag camp near the Mongolian border. Martin Connolly left the house to his sister, Maureen and her daughter. Mrs. Burke told Nina that they left the farm shortly after and went back to England. The house was now deserted and run down.

Kevin Burke and Nina pushed through the old front door that hung on one hinge. The rooms were all dirty and covered with soot. Somehow, Nina felt an urge to explore each room individually. She started to pick up different pieces of broken pottery and seemed fascinated with the discovery. Some of the furniture lay broken on the floor. She tried to stand these pieces on their legs. Burke noticed she was in a daze. Finally, Burke moved over to her and stopped her from picking up any more items on the floor. "Please," he said, "you are doing no good here. Everything is in ruins." Nina looked at him. It was a pitiful look. "This is my house," and with that she sunk to the floor, sobbing. Burke couldn't believe his eyes. He had watched this woman kill a man without giving it a thought. She assassinated Margaret Watson, and now she was showing him a side of her he never dreamed possible. Burke had no idea how close she was to the edge of a breakdown. Burke was not aware of the deep emotions she experienced at meeting her mother not too long ago. Major Kislaik was the only one that was aware of her fragile mental condition.

Nina was slowly losing the hate defense that she had hung on to for years. It was the only protection she had against the outside world. Raised without parents in a home with sadistic and cruel individuals that helped train her for her job as a assassin for the KGB. Suddenly, her own actions had been called in question. Her only reason to live was to kill the people she was told to.

Nina was now experiencing love and warmth from her love with Kevin Burke. She found a feeling of affection for her father, Martin Connolly. She could not assassinate him. Finally, the warmth of her mother's arms around her still remained in her memory.

All these emotions flowing into Nina's brain at once was too much for her. Wave after wave of emotions exploded in her head. Suddenly, she experienced an overload in her brain. She became lost and confused.

Nina collapsed on the floor. Burke tried to lift her from her fall but to no avail. She didn't move. He finally got her to sit up on the floor but she started to cry and make strange noises that sounded like chanting. After a little while, he picked her up and carried her to the car. Burke drove straight to the Galway City Hospital. After waiting for about two hours, a doctor approached him and told him that it was too early to determine her condition. The doctor continued, "Nina has lapsed into a state of unawareness. She doesn't know where she is or who she is. I have experienced this type of case before. They rarely come out of it. It is much too early to make any prediction one way or the other. I have given you the worse scenario so that you will not build your hopes up."

"My God!" Burke shouted out and at the same time grabbed hold of the doctor's lapels and threw him against the wall. "What are you saying to me? Nina will never be the same again?"

The doctor asked him quickly to calm down. He understood what Burke was feeling. "I am sorry," Burke said. "It's just that I love her so. I can't believe I am hearing this. She was so strong, vibrant and beautiful. What can I do?" Burke pleaded.

"Nothing," the doctor replied. "Get some rest and leave a telephone number where you can be reached."

Leaving the hospital, Burke was in a state of deep depression. How he missed her already. When he reached his mother's house, he sunk down on the living room chair. Mother and son talked until the break of day. He told her of Nina's collapse and that Nina was in the Galway hospital in a coma. The next day, Burke was ordered back to America. He never told his mother he was leaving Ireland. Mrs. Burke believed he was still in Galway.

***

Three days had passed and no word from Nina. Major Kisliak was concerned about his agent. Colonel Zaitsev would be making inquiries about Nina. She could be in some trouble, although it was a simple assignment to deliver the 20,000 pounds to the agents. Maybe customs discovered it and rather than act then and there, trailed Nina to see if she might lead them to some IRA activity. She could also have been held for questioning. It was not like Nina not to follow proper procedure. Kisliak started checking out different dispatches from England and Ireland and found nothing. While going through the different reports on foreign agents in Ireland, he noted a small notation identifying a CIA agent named Kevin Burke's arrival in Dublin a few days before the disappearance of Nina. The American Embassy in Dublin was constantly watched by the KGB agent to keep track of American agents entering the premises. Burke was spotted and identified by Moscow. The American Intelligence Agency does the same in Moscow. Kisliak informed Colonel Zaitsev that Nina might be in some trouble.

Kisliak knew that the colonel would not approve a high-ranking officer like himself to fly to Ireland to investigate an agent that was missing. The minute he landed in Ireland, the CIA agents would identify him. So Kisliak came up with a logical reason for him to go to Ireland. The Russian Tourist Ministry had a group leaving for Dublin the following week. It was to be an exchange group touring Ireland. It was sponsored by the Russian Government. The Irish government has the same program in force. They, too, would sponsor a group of Irish citizens touring Russia the following month. It was to exchange their cultures and to get acquainted with their respective countries.

Kisliak convinced Zaitsev to let him go with the Russian touring group as one of the Russian citizens. He would be thoroughly disguised with a false passport and documents. Before Kisliak left the Colonel's office, the Colonel caught hold of his arm. He said, "Be careful that you don't get too involved with this agent."

Kislaik pretended to laugh, "I'm old enough to be her grandfather."

"Maybe so," said Zaitsev, "but you seem overly concerned about her welfare."

Major Kisliak made note that Zaitsev was on to him and there could be no more special favors for Nina or himself. The following week, Major Boris Kisliak was on a plane to Dublin, Ireland with the tour group. After landing in Dublin Airport and passing though immigration and customs, he slipped away from the group. Kisliak took a taxi to the same hotel that Nina was staying at in the center of town. He went immediately to his room after checking in. He returned to the lobby at about 4 am in the morning. Kisliak, being an old hand at covert activities, knew from experience that the night porter is usually asleep at that time. The lobby was deserted. Kislaik went behind the Front Desk and accessed the hotel's computer. It had the names of all the guests. Nina was listed for room 404. He immediately turned off the computer.

Kisliak took the stairs up to the fourth floor to room 404. It was no problem for a KGB agent to unlock the room door. He stepped into the dark room and turned on a small flashlight. After searching the room quietly but methodically, he found Nina's suitcase. Placing the suitcase on the bed, he proceeded to look inside of the lining of the bag. The 20,000 pounds were still intact. Why after three days hadn't she passed the money on to the agents? There seemed to be no clothes missing. But not knowing what she had actually taken with her, he was guessing. There was no clue in the room to where she has gone. Kisliak left Nina's room and returned to his own. No one had seen him come or go.

Kislaik was awakened by the sun shining in his window. He lazily rose from his bed and like most men his age, cursed the pain from his arthritis. Facing the mirror in the morning, Major Boris Kisliak was a miserable man. One look at his appearance made him wish he was back in bed. Oh, those age spots and thinning hair brought him back to reality. "Retire, you old bastard," he said quietly to himself. "This game is not for you anymore." While standing under the shower, a flash came to him. There was a good chance Nina went to see her father's home in Galway. It was the only lead he could follow up on.

Later that day, to make sure he wasn't going down to Galway for nothing, he made contact with the agents who she had been going to pass the money to. The agents informed him that they had had no word from her. He then checked in with the Russian Embassy in Dublin. There he met with the station chief for the KGB just over from London on other business. The chief informed Kisliak that he had a report from Dublin from one of his agents that saw a KGB agent make contact with a CIA agent in Dublin. "Do you recall his name?" Kisliak asked. "Yes," he replied, "it was a Kevin Burke. We have known about him for a while. He was seen with a young lady who we later we identified as Nina Garcia."

After returning to the hotel, Kisliak stood in front of the mirror. He checked his appearance. He had on a dress shirt and tie that was covered by his light blue sports jacket, and a soft felt hat. He stepped back from the mirror and thought, *Not too bad for an old guy.* His rented car heads down the Galway road. He was in Galway in 3.5 hours. Going through Connemara, he made inquiries about the Connolly house. After receiving directions, he set out for the old house. By pure chance, he found Kevin Burke's home on the way to Martin Connolly's house. Kisliak decided to stop for directions. He knew that he was close but it was possible that he had passed it.

The major left his car and knocked on the old wood door. After a little while, an old lady came to the door. "Yes," she said in a very cheerful voice. "Can I help you?" Kisliak didn't want to appear inquisitive so he asked for a glass of water. "Come in, come in," said the old woman. She appeared to be glad to see him. "Listen," she said, "You look tired. I will make you a nice cup of tea and then you can be on your way." Kisliak couldn't help but smile at this woman. It was as though she had known him all his life. "My son just came from America a few days ago," she told him. "He has a big job in Washington, D.C. you know, and he brought this beautiful girl with him. She was absolutely stunning." Kisliak inquired if she was American. "Oh no, she was half Spanish and would you believe that the other half was Irish. Sure her father's house is just down the road from here. I knew him all his life. Isn't that strange? There was a terrible tragedy that happened to her in her father's house. She is in the hospital in Galway City."

"Oh yes," said Kislaik. He sounded like the cat that swallowed the canary. He proceeded with some small talk and then he thanked the old woman for her hospitality. When he was getting into his car, she said to him, "The direction you are heading in is on the way to where my son's girlfriend's house is located. It belonged to her father, Martin Connolly. Please if you hear anything about Kevin along the way, get back to me as I'm worried. I haven't heard from him in two days."

"I will do just that, Madam."

"Oh," she said, "I hope I did not bore you with my son and his girlfriend."

Major Kisliak looked at her with a smile, "Madam, you will never know what your conversation meant to me."

Checking out Martin Connolly's home, he found it to be empty. It looked like someone had been there recently. The house hadn't been lived in for years. Kisliak noticed signs of cobwebs being disturbed and footprints on the dusty floors.

Kisliak got in his car and headed to Galway City. There he would check the hospital to see if she was still there. Kisliak stood outside of the Galway City Hospital and studied the entrances and exits in and out of the hospital. He pondered the best way of getting her out. Finally, he went inside and went directly to the admitting desk. He noticed that the visiting hours were only a few minutes away. So, he decided to do his searching with the visitors.

The hospital was fairly large and it would take Kislaik some time to locate Nina's room. He couldn't just make an inquiry at the desk. The chance was that Burke might have some of his people watching her room. It would not do to get careless because of his anxiety over her. If he was careful he could find her today without causing any suspicion. A group of visitors stood in front of the elevator and were given the signal to go to the rooms. Kislaik slipped into the elevator and he got off at the first floor and started walking past the patient's rooms. The floor was crowded with visitors. He moved around without drawing any attention to himself. After about 20 minutes, he had thoroughly searched the entire first floor. Taking the stairs up to the second floor, he proceeded to do the same. Kisliak had covered about half of the second floor when he came to a room that was closed and outside the door was a stocky young man in his twenties that was guarding the room. Kisliak walked by the room and appeared to be looking farther down the hall for another room. Kisliak recognized immediately that the young man was an Irish policeman in civilian clothes, not a CIA man.

In the late afternoon, Kisliak had stopped in a Galway City hotel to take supper. There he contacted the KGB station in Dublin. He was assigned two men and a van to bring Nina to the airport and out of the country. The next evening after the agents arrived in Galway city, he briefed them. Kisliak then set off for the hospital. They would take her out during visitor's hours. Kisliak parked the van at the side exit of the hospital. The biggest problem was the Irish policeman. Kisliak decided to handle the guard himself. The two agents would remove Nina from the bed and put her in a laundry cart that collected soiled linens and sheets. The day before Kisliak had located a large laundry cart close to Nina's room. While he was searching the first floor, he located a room with doctor's medical attire. He took three outfits with him out of the hospital in a carry-on bag.

The three men entered the hospital and went immediately to the men's room where they changed into the doctors' medical attire. They took different elevators to Nina's room on the second floor. Kisliak left the elevator at the second floor and walked quickly to Nina's room. The guard was sitting in a chair reading a newspaper. He looked up briefly at Kisliak as he passed his chair to enter Nina's room. There was no hesitation on Kisliak's part as he struck the guard on the side of his neck. The guard fell to the ground. The other two men were in the room with the cart. In seconds, Kisliak pulled the unconscious policeman by his legs into the room. The other two agents worked quickly. They put Nina into the cart and covered her with sheets and pillowcases and soiled towels. Kislaik noticed that Nina was unconscious, and the tears began to form in his dark eyes, unusual for this hardcore KGB man. They reached the side entrance in minutes and Nina was placed in the van and on her way without the slightest intervention. They proceeded to drive directly to Shannon Airport. She was brought to the freight department where she was concealed in a freight shipment to Moscow. They then loaded it on an Aeroflot flight. The Russians were experts at smuggling people out of countries to Moscow.

The following day, Major Boris Kislaik was in uniform waiting for Colonel Zaitsev in his office. The colonel sat down at his desk but didn't give Kisliak permission to sit. This let

Kisliak know the colonel wasn't too happy with him. The colonel raised up his head and looked directly into Kisliak's eyes. "What the hell is going on with you and this woman? The way you have handled this agent would lead me to believe you are involved with her. What I do know is that you are acting like an old fool with this girl and that is the only reason I believe there is nothing else behind this. Major Kisliak, you have been a good soldier and a loyal communist. So, I will order you to spend no more time with this agent. I want her shipped out at once to one of the gulag camps."

Kisliak turned white, "My Colonel," he said. "She is sick and in a coma. We can't do that to her. Nina has done fine work for us. This would look very bad for us with our other agents."

Colonel Zaitsev said, "I have here in my desk a report from our station chief in England that indicates she was seeing a CIA agent in Ireland. Major Kisliak, your name was mentioned as making inquiries about her movements in Ireland. I believe she has gone over to the CIA and the only reason you are standing here in front of me and not in a gulag camp is that I don't believe you were aware of her liaison with this CIA agent."

"My Colonel," Major Kisliak answered, "you are aware that I went to Ireland to find out what happened to her."

Zaitsev shouted out at Kisliak, "You are an old fool in love with a young, beautiful woman and it has blinded you to her deception. I want her to disappear. If this is found out, that we were deceived by her, the center will have us both shot. I want the CIA to find out that she is dead. Do you understand me Major?"

Kisliak could see it was no use talking any more to Zaitsev. "Which gulag will I send her to?" he asked.

"I don't give a damn where!" Zaitsev shouted back. "Listen, you damn fool," Zaitsev continued, "she won't last a week in one of those camps. She is in a coma. That means she will be sent to the hospital in the camp and you know the excellent record the Gulag camps have for survival in one these hospitals. Now get out of here before I decide to send you with her. Major Kisliak, you have put me in great danger with your involvement with this woman. All the years you and I have spent together has saved you from the firing squad. Please go now!"

Kisliak sat at his desk and typed Nina's name on all the necessary papers. After he had filled in the all the proper forms, he left them with Zaitsev that afternoon. The papers were returned to him with Colonel Zaitsev's signature on them. They were in duplicate. Kislaik was sending Nina according to her papers to Gulag Camp 6. The duplicate copy was to be signed by the commandant of the camp and returned to Zaitsev's office. Kisliak was going to have Nina delivered to her mother's camp, Gulag 8. Kisliak knew that her mother Contessa would take care of her in the camp's hospital. This would give him some time to work out a plan to get Nina away from the camp. The change in the camp's number would throw any investigation off. Kisliak would have her delivered to the Gulag Camp 8.

The two copies signed by Colonel Zaitsev had Gulag Camp 6 on them. When Nina arrived at Gulag Camp 8, Kislaik would have the commandant presented with both copies but the top copy would have been changed from Gulag 6 to Gulag 8. It was Kislaik's hope that the commandant would quickly sign the receipt without spotting the bottom carbon copy he was returning to Ziatsev which was for Gulag 6. Kislaik believed that Zaitsev, receiving the signed copy, would be convinced that Nina was safely in the hands of Gulag Camp 6. This would give Kislaik time to get Nina safely out of Gulag 8.

To complete this, he needed someone he could trust to get Nina to Gulag Camp 8. He made a call to an old comrade he had served with in World War II. His name was Sergei Leonov. Leonov was an ex-Russian Air Force Captain and an Ace in World War II and he now was flying with an air show in Moscow. Kislaik met with him that evening at an old drinking place they once inhabited years ago. After exchanging the usual pleasantries, Kislaik explained his plan to him. Leonov was always one to play the odds. If he was found out, it was the gulag camp for him. "My God, I love the intrigue," said Leonov. "This is the best proposition I have received in years." He would pick up Nina, fly her to the camp and present the papers to the commandant. He would then return the copy back to Kislaik who would present it as proof that Nina was in Camp 6. The old friend made the arrangements to meet him in a deserted air strip outside of Moscow. Kislaik delivered Nina to Leonov, who flew her to the Gulag Camp 8. She was still in a coma. A few days later, Leonov met with Kislaik at the same drinking place and they toasted each other. It had gone off just fine. The Commandant had never noticed what he was signing.

That night Leonov and Kislaik got drunk and ended up in a house of prostitution. Kislaik would now have to come up with a good plan to get Nina safely away from the camp. By now, Kislaik knew he was very much in love with Nina. He remembered when the plane lifted off; he felt a loneliness that he had never experienced before.

When Nina arrived at Gulag 8, she was immediately transferred to the camp hospital. Contessa Garcia, her mother, realized that she was the girl that came to the camp awhile back. She knew and felt it was her lost baby returned to her. Leonov slipped her a note from Kislaik explaining the whole situation. Shortly afterward, the commandant appeared. He gave Contessa an order not to waste any time or extra food on this woman. She was of no importance. They had pawned her off in his camp. Evidently someone high up wanted to get rid of her, she was probably someone's mistress.

***

Langley, VA

Kevin Burke sat quietly while the Assistant Director of Operations chewed on his ear. "Kevin, you damn fool. Falling for this girl is endangering this valuable source of intelligence. What the hell is wrong with you? Then you lose her to the KGB. Well, I'm waiting for an answer." Kevin Burke got up from his chair and walked over to the window. He turned and faced the director, "I can't help it. This happens in this business once in awhile, doesn't it?"

"Yes," the director answered back. "Somehow I don't recall anyone making such a mess out of an important operation as big as this one over one woman. This girl's information was as good as it gets. She identified moles for us, who were working in this office for our assistant director. They were privy to all intelligence related to that department. There is no doubt in my mind that she has contact with someone at a high level in the KGB." Burke just stared at him. The director placed his forefinger in Burke's face. "Get out of here and find her. I don't want to see you again until you have her in the USA." Kevin Burke took his leave from the director.

The following week in Galway, Ireland, Burke returned to his home in Connemara for his first real visit in a long time. When he had come last time with Nina, it was only for a night. He had taken Nina to see her father's house but he returned another night to his mother's to tell her what had happened at the Connolly house. After reporting the situation to the CIA, he was ordered to return to Washington immediately. Burke never went back to his house. He just went straight to Shannon Airport and on to Washington, D.C. When Burke returned to Ireland, Mrs. Burke opened the door and couldn't believe her eyes. Kevin was back and so soon. She couldn't believe it. The Irish mother loves her sons dearly. It is not that she has less feeling for her daughters but somehow there is a special kind of extra feelings for her man child. "Oh, Mrs. Burke," he said, placing his arms around her waist. "It is you that warms the cockles of my heart." Mrs. Burke's face turned red, "Go away with yourself. I would hate to have to count the number of your lassies you said that too." Burke lifted her up in the air and then sat down with her on his lap. "Tell me woman, have you had any proposals since I seen you last." Mrs. Burke threw her head back and started to laugh. Suddenly she put her hands on his face and looked into his eyes. She lowered his head next to the side of her face. Burke felt the tears run down the side of his face. Any man that has an Irish born mother knows that emotion for them ends quickly and the next order of the day is, "You look thin. I'm going to make you tea." Tea usually consists of a full course dinner and you'd better finish it.

While Burke was sitting at the table eating his mother's fine cooking, she mentioned the stranger that came to her house not too long after he left. Burke asked her to describe him. She said he was a foreigner with a funny accent she had never heard. After she finished dinner, she continued to tell Burke what a lovely man he was. A real gentleman she said. Burke couldn't help but smile. He had figured out who your man was, as they would say in Ireland. The next morning he left for Galway City to go to the hospital. After discovering Nina was not there, he made inquiries with the Hospital Administrator. Then he went directly to check out Nina's room. He personally interviewed the nurses who were on duty the day Nina was reported missing. No one knew how she disappeared. Finally Burke stopped a young man pushing a laundry cart with soiled linens. The young man had witnessed two men pushing a linen cart to the hospital exit. He also saw them remove a large bag which looked heavy and loaded it into a van. Burke asked him why he hadn't reported this to his supervisors. "Listen sir," he replied to Burke, "down here, we mind our own business." Burke threw his arms up in the air and walked out of the hospital. He drove straight to Shannon Airport. Kevin Burke checked at the airport with the Russian airline and found out a Russian airplane took off from Shannon a few hours after she had been kidnapped from the hospital. The destination was Moscow.

Kevin Burke knew now that somewhere in Moscow they had Nina. How would he find her? That night he sat at a Limerick bar and drank till closing.

Gulag Camp 8

At the Gulag camp, Contessa Garcia was caring for Nina the best she could, even sharing with Nina the small rations she received at the camp, desperately trying to keep Nina alive. The commandant was a constant threat. He would appear from time to time. "We are wasting good food on this corpse," he would say.

Chapter 11

Kevin Burke in Moscow

The next day in Dublin, Kevin Burke had lunch with McManus, the CIA station chief who operated out of London. He flew over from London with CIA files on the Russians who operated in Ireland. After lunch, they went to St. Stephen's Green Park off Grafton Street and sat on one of the empty benches that were strung along the park. McManus pointed out to Burke one of the files, which was of a Major Boris Kisliak. He was a high-ranking officer in the KGB. His rank was deceiving. He was the assistant to Colonel Zaitsev, who was head of the Illegal Directorate in Moscow. "So, what has this KGB officer to do with Nina Garcia?" Burke asked. McManus answered him. "This gentleman landed in Ireland a week after you met Nina in Dublin. We believe this is her control." McManus continued, "If you want to find Nina you will have to get to him. No easy task. There is no other way."

Burke knew that Langley would not approve of his going to Moscow. They believed he was emotionally involved with Nina. Kevin Burke was carrying enough papers on him to give a reason for his trip to Moscow. He was also carrying his Irish passport. Burke had once worked for an Irish tool company in Goatstown, Dublin before he went to America. After becoming an American citizen, he had joined the CIA. This Irish company had a representative in Moscow. His name was Danny Murphy.

Burke met him in Moscow when he was sent over to bring Murphy up to speed on a new toll line the company was trying to sell the Russians.

On a warm Dublin day Kevin Burke met with Michael Rafferty, the managing director of this Irish tool company, for a few drinks at a local pub that the employees from the tool company would stop into after work. Burke had been well liked when he worked there. Rafferty was delighted to see him and they downed a few pints together. Burke informed Rafferty that he was now living in America and he had made some strong contacts with an American company. Among the items they were exporting to Russia were American tools. Burke told Rafferty that the business was worth millions of dollars. "What I would like to propose to you is that you temporarily hire me at 10% commission to move your line of tools with the Russians. I would only need some expenses to cover my fare to Moscow, and a hotel room for few days. The necessary company authorizations in writing and some ID that I work for the company would be required." Rafferty jumped at the offer. He knew what Burke was capable of doing. He had been the leading sales representative when he had worked for the Irish tool company.

Burke met with Rafferty in his office a week later, and he was given the necessary papers and documents. A business visa and a letter of introduction from the Managing Director Michael Rafferty were furnished for Burke. Burke was on his way.

Burke had no problems getting by Russian Immigration at the Moscow Airport. He went immediately to the Moscow hotel. The same hotel Nina had stayed at when he met her in Moscow for a briefing. He remembered the room number she had been in and asked the clerk for the same room. It was vacant and Burke booked it. When he entered the room, it brought back flashes of Nina standing in front of him. He remembered how beautiful she was. Burke had not forgotten that night. She wore a tight light blue blouse and black short skirt. She was, as they say in Ireland, a knock out. The room became lonely and cool. The light from Nina being there had disappeared. He sat on a chair looking out at the dark cool night in Moscow.

After breakfast the next morning, he went through a Moscow directory and found the names of several Russian tool distributors. He wired Michael Rafferty at the Irish tool Company that he would be calling on them. This was to throw off suspicion. He knew his wire would be looked at by the KGB. Any businessman entering Russia was generally under suspicion. Burke found two such companies not too far from where Major Kisliak's office was located. Burke phoned Danny Murray, the representative of the Irish tool company, and made an appointment with him to meet at a local Moscow restaurant. The Dublin man met him with a big smile and informed him that Rafferty had filled him in on what Burke intended to do. Burke was used to deceiving people, but this time it was his own kind and he felt badly because the excited Murray was hoping for big sales. Danny Murray arranged to give him a company car, with samples and brochures to help him move the Irish tool company's line of products.

Two days later, Burke was driving around Moscow. Burke had stopped his car on a street that was not far from Major Boris Kisliak's office. He was studying photos of Kisliak, which he had received from MacManus in Ireland. When Kisliak appeared, he was going to his office. It was 8:05 am. The following morning he spotted Kisliak again at about 8:05 am going to his office. That evening Burked left his hotel. It was about 1 am in the morning. He parked his car two blocks from a Russian pub. He left his car and walked to the pub. Burke stood in front of the pub's window and looked in. It was nearly empty except for three Russian soldiers drinking at a table. The three soldiers were drunk. Burke waited in the shadows of the pub. About 2:30 am, two soldiers appeared and continued on their way to a parked car that was not too far from the pub. The night was cold and Burke was starting to feel it. He must have smoked a half pack of cigarettes while waiting in the dark night. Finally, the last soldier from the pub appeared and Burke could see he was barely able to walk. The soldier passed by Burke and at that moment, Burke sprung out at him, knocking him unconscious. He quickly stripped him of his uniform and ID that was in his tunic pocket.

The following morning, parked in the street where Kisliak's office was located, Burke waited patiently for him. He saw Kisliak coming down the street. He was walking with about five or six civilians who appeared to be going to work themselves. As the group passed the car, Burke came out of the car and stood at attention as Kisliak walked by. He quietly opened the car door as if he was waiting for Kisliak. The group had passed by, hardly glancing at the car. Just as Kislaik stood to look at Burke, Burke moved towards him. Burke placed his pistol in Kisliak's stomach, "Get in the car now." Kisliak had no time to react so he went directly into the passenger's front seat of the car. Burke sat next to him. "If you want to see another Russian day, you will do exactly what I tell you." Kisliak smiled at him. He knew who he was. "Yes, Mr. Burke," he said. "You will have not trouble from me." Burke couldn't believe what he was hearing. Burke started the car, his right hand on the steering wheel and his left hand pointing his gun at Kisliak's stomach which was hidden under his right arm. They drove about 20 miles outside Moscow to a wooded area. When he ordered Kisliak out of the car, they walked into the woods where Burke forced Kisliak to sit down on a large fallen tree. Burke looked down at Kisliak, who seemed quite relaxed. Burke's brain was buzzing. "How do you know who I am?" Burke asked. Kisliak asked if he could light his pipe. Burke nodded his head. As he watched, Kisliak lit his pipe and made himself as comfortable as one could on a fallen tree, Burke was impressed with the coolness of this Major Boris Kisliak. After drawing in a pipe full of smoke, Kisliak exhaled it as if he was at home relaxing after a good meal. "My dear Mr. Burke, I know you are Nina Garcia's lover and her controller for the CIA."

Burke was studying Kisliak as he spoke. Burke remained silent for a while and then asked Kisliak, "How long have you known about Nina and me?"

"One evening in her hotel in Moscow, she broke down and told me everything."

"So, you have been using her to get to me," Burke said.

"No, no, my friend. You are not the only one to fall in love with Nina."

Burke started to smile. Kisliak turned red and with anger said, "Do not smile at me. I may be old but I am still a man. Nina knew I was in love with her from the first time I saw her. She convinced me to turn over the names of the moles in your organization. It was not hard to do after many years, I was disgusted with the system and I was so in love with Nina, I would do anything for her." Burke knew he was telling the truth. Only someone in Kisliak's position would have been able to give Nina those names. Burke asked where Nina was now. He received a negative answer and Burke lost his temper and struck Kisliak across the mouth with the back of his hand. Kisliak fell off the fallen tree and wiped the blood from his mouth. He rose to his feet.

"I will tell you where she is," Kisliak replied. "I'm getting too old for this kind of work." Kisliak told Burke where Nina was and gave him all the details of how she got there. Then Burke grew angry, "How could you send a sick girl to a Gulag camp?" He struck Kisliak again, this time with a punch to Kisliak's gut, knocking him to the ground. Burke pulled him up from the ground and threw him up against a tree. Burke put his pistol to Kisliak's head, "I'm going to kill you, you SOB." Kisliak grabbed the pistol and struggled with Burke till both men fell to the ground. Major Boris Kisliak had over 35 years on Burke but he was a strong man. Kisliak managed to turn Burke's gun hand into his chest and at the same time, pull Burke's trigger finger, firing a shot into Burke's chest. Burke rolled over on the ground and lay still. Kisliak rose to his feet. He threw Burke's body over an embankment and drove away. Kisliak knew that with winter coming, the snow would soon hide Burke's body. No one would ever find him. He had taken Burke's Irish passport and all the documents that would have explained how he got into Russia. He knew if Nina ever came out of her comma, he could never tell her what happened to Burke.

He drove back to his office, where he changed his dirty and bloody uniform. Kisliak sat the rest of the day at his desk, staring out the window into the Moscow's streets.

Chapter 12

Major Kisliak had betrayed his country and knew that he was on his way to Gulag Camp 8 to rescue his love, Nina. The major had received no word on how Contessa Garcia and her daughter were doing for months. He wondered if Nina was still alive. He could not sit in Moscow, knowing she was in that death camp.

Major Kisliak looked out at the frozen landscape through the train window and saw his reflection. He asked himself how this all happened. His thoughts wandered back to that day when Nina came into Lt. Colonel Zaitsev's office. The moment he saw her, he had fallen in love with her. She was young and beautiful and she awoke a deep passion in him that he had not experienced in years. Her face appeared in the train window to him but quickly faded into the night. The face was replaced with that of his wife of 45 years, Sonia.

He was just 21 years old when he married her. She was a plump and ugly woman. He frowned into the train window. He could barely look at her. He removed his hat and actually found himself sweating. The wind was blowing so hard that he could feel the cold air entering the closed train windows. The snow had gathered momentum and was coming down heavy. He continued to stare out the window and from time to time, he would see his reflection. Sonia's father was a general in the KGB, which was the reason Kisliak had advanced from KGB border guard to a major in the First Chief Directorate's Office under Lt. Colonel Zaitsev. He was picked to join the honorary guards at 21 years of age. They were the guards who escorted top KGB generals to state functions at the Kremlin. Sonia's father, a KGB general, was being escorted to a function one evening. He brought his daughter to the affair. When the general and his daughter were dancing, she pointed to Kisliak, who was standing guard at one of the entrances. Later the General came over to Kisliak and requested him to dance with his daughter. Kisliak had not noticed the general's daughter when they were dancing. When he finally approached her, his first reaction was to run, but he knew that the old general would have him posted in Siberia, so he made the best of it. While they were dancing, she kept squeezing his arm till he thought the circulation would never come back. Kisliak smiled in the window.

Sonia had her father transfer Kisliak to his office in the First Chief Directorate. Kisliak had no formal education but was still promoted to clerk. The General had hired a tutor for him and he was taking courses at night to help him with his duties in the office. This did not come without a price. Sonia kept demanding dates with him and soon it became a situation that Kisliak couldn't get out of. One morning the general called him into his office; he was all smiles and asked the young man to sit down. "My daughter tells me that you are a very respectful young man who has made no attempt to seduce her. I find this refreshing in this day and age." Once again, Kisliak smiled into the window when he thought to himself he would have rather seduced a baboon. "Since you get along so well with my daughter then I can assume that we will be seeing a wedding coming up shortly." Kisliak jumped up from the seat, "No, No sir. I think you have misunderstood my intentions. I take your daughter out only to be polite." He had barely got the words out of his mouth when the general roared like a wounded bear. "Sit down, sit down you insect. My dear Kisliak, you have but two choices. A lovely wedding and a very secure future with the KGB or I will personally have you arrested for seducing my daughter. I believe the penalty would be 20 years in a Gulag prison in Siberia. What my daughter failed to tell you was that she is only 15 years of age. She looks much older. That was your mistake not to find out the small details." Kisliak turned white, "But sir you know that this is not true."

"Oh yes," said the good general, "but whose word would the court take, yours or mine, a distinguished general with an excellent war record or a worm like you?"

The General stood up, "Please make the necessary arrangements with my daughter. Good afternoon, private." Kisliak remembered leaving the general's office. He could hardly stand up. His legs felt like rubber.

Kisliak turned from the train window and put his head between his legs. He opened up the collar of his military coat for once again he began sweating. Kisliak was married the following month. The bride wore white and Kisliak wore his brand new lieutenant's uniform. He had been made a commissioned officer by Daddy. This promotion went through a week before the wedding. The honeymoon was a disaster. When he first saw Sonia on their wedding bed, he threw up. Many years later, the good general died and Colonel Zaitsev became head of the department. By then, Kisliak had been made a major. He would never go any further at that rank as long as Colonel Zaitsev remained in place. That night in the Moscow hotel with Nina had become the happiest time he had experienced in 35 years. She stole his soul and he agreed to work with her to give the CIA the names of the moles that had infiltrated the FBI and CIA.

A few hours later, Kisliak got off the train and hired a car to get to the Gulag camp.

Chapter 13

The major introduced himself to the commandant, and to his surprise he found that the commandant he had met when he had brought Nina to see her mother had been replaced. This man was not the typical individual that ran this sort of camp. Lt. Colonel Drozdov was an educated man with a sense of decency about him. Kisliak explained that his presence in the camp was due to the severe weather, which forced him to find shelter in the nearby camp.

The commandant was a gracious host, and that night they had a late dinner. They talked most of the night about their experiences in the war. During the dinner, Kisliak expressed his interest in the camp and asked if he might take a tour of the camp. The commandant would arrange this in the morning.

Major Kisliak was given an accommodation for the night. The next morning he rose with a hangover he had received during the night, in the good commandant's company. Kisliak had a difficult time controlling himself. He was concerned that he would not find Nina there. The commandant assigned one of his guards to escort the major on his tour of the camp. After a boring first part of the morning, he finally got into the hospital. He searched frantically with his eyes to find Nina. There was no sign of Contessa Garcia or Nina. Did he come in vain?

Trying his best to seem calm, he told the guard he had been here before on official business. He was hoping the guard would not mention this to the commandant. "I brought in a prisoner named Nina Garcia. Is she still here?" The guard was trying to place Nina and to the best of his memory, he thought she was dead. "Our nurse would know, but she's with a mobile unit that travels to the Gulag camps in this area. She left awhile back." He had no idea when she would return. Kisliak felt weak in the knees, the first part of the guard's words, that he thought she was dead, left him cold all over. What could he do now? He could not remain in the Gulag camp for long.

Once again he took a risk by mentioning Nina in conversation with the commandant. He was sitting in the commandant's office and they were discussing his tour when he laughingly told the commandant that a guard told him that there was a beautiful woman patient here but he thought she was dead. "I suppose," he said to the commandant "that you don't get to see too many pretty women come in here." He was trying desperately to engage the commandant in conversation of a trivial nature. He knew that anyone who had seen Nina would not have forgotten her. "Oh yes," said the commandant "I do remember seeing her, but she's not dead. Her name was Nina. Somehow I do not remember her last name. The guard was right, she was beautiful." Kisliak broke out in a sweat. The commandant used the word 'was.' It seemed to Kisliak to be hours, waiting for the commandant to continue the conversation. Kisliak was about to lead him back to what happened to Nina when one of the guards came into the room to speak to him about some incident that happened that day. Kisliak by now was slowly breaking down, his hope had faded and he was in the deepest turmoil. How would he bring back the commandant to that same conversation without arousing his suspicion?

Kisliak breathed a sigh of relief when the commandant brought the conversation back to Nina. "Our nurse here took her on her mobile operation. She said she needed her for an assistant." Major Kisliak sat back in the chair. Did the commandant say they took Nina with the nurse? This would mean that Nina was out of the coma. Once again he had to bite his tongue to not be too inquisitive about Nina. His heart was beating faster and he could feel his pulse beating in his wrist. Kisliak was trying to lead the commandant into some specific answers about Nina. Kisliak remarked, "This girl? What did you say her name was? Nina? Was she a nurse too?" "No," the commandant said, "in fact she was a patient that had been in a coma. And our own nurse brought her out of it. It was an outstanding accomplishment." The major felt reborn again. He was capable of jumping over the moon and kept saying to himself, *She's well again! She's well again!*

Kisliak soon settled down, "Well, I must be on my way. I thank you for your hospitality and I will be delighted to put in a favorable word for you with the center." The commandant was overjoyed with Kisliak's promise.

When Kisliak stepped out of the commandant's building he was met with a blast of cold air, mixed with snow. It woke him up and it reminded him, "How am I going to get her out of here?" A guard stood at attention and opened the door of his car. Kisliak spoke for a few minutes to the guard about his family. He asked if he knew the nurse at the camp. "Oh yes," the soldier replied. "She is a fine nurse and she is attached to the mobile unit. After a while the soldier remembered that the nurses were going to Gulag camp 9, which was not too far from there. And they would be returning tomorrow night.

Kisliak had driven about 20 miles when he stopped at a house that seemed isolated and was covered in snow and ice. He waited for a few minutes in the blinding snow, finally he knocked on the door. The door opened and an old man appeared and pushed Kisliak into the house. The man shouted, "Come in, come in! You'll get us all frozen to death." The room was small and it was lit only by a small candle in the middle of a large table. The table was so big it nearly took up the whole room.

After removing his coat and hat he looked for some form of heat. There in the middle of the room was a small fireplace with a large fire burning brightly. Kisliak looked around the room and there was a small shelf of books against the wall. A tray of half-eaten food was on the big table. Two chairs were behind the table and Kisliak sat down and lit his pipe. Kisliak then concentrated on the old man. "How far are you away from the train station?" he asked. "About 60 miles," the old man replied. "Do you live alone here?" Kisliak asked, "Yes," said the old man. "How do you get along out here so far from anyone?" "Oh, I manage," the old man said, "the wood is plenty around here. I receive supplies from the camp down the road. One of the guards brings me my supplies once a month."

"Why do you live here alone? Surely this is not your home?"

"I was a prisoner at Gulag camp 8 for 20 years, and when I was released I found this old deserted house and I've been living in it since."

Kisliak asked the old man if he could stay for the night. The old man said he would be delighted for his company. Kisliak sat back after a modest super which mostly consisted of chopped up beef and potatoes. It was quite delicious. After super, Kisliak smoked his pipe and spoke quietly to the old man. "I have a mistress who I would like to bring here for a short time. She has broken a minor law but it is not that serious. I do not wish the authorities to connect her to me. I'm in a very sensitive position in the government. I'm sure you understand."

"Oh yes," the old man replied. "I can see you're a man of substance and some importance." The old man thought for a moment and then he brought forth an observation. "There is very little room here for three people, how would we arrange the accommodations?" Kisliak smiled at the old man "I'm prepared to compensate you for your trouble." Tomorrow morning, I will drive you to the train that will take you to Moscow and I will give you enough rubles to stay in a hotel in Moscow for about two months. I will also pay for any expenses you may incur when staying in Moscow." Kisliak was watching the old man's face when he saw a doubt come over it. Kisliak continued "and I will also give you a substantial amount of rubles for your trouble." The old man's face showed him that his offer was accepted. If he hadn't taken the offer Kisliak would have had to kill him and he didn't want to do that.

That night as Kisliak slept in the old man's bed, his mind was at ease for the first time in months. The old man slept next to him in the bed and even the old man's snoring didn't distract him from his sleep.

Kisliak rose early the next morning and bundled the old man into his car. It took him four hours to go 60 miles to the old railroad station. The weather struck out at him like an old wounded bear. It was merciless. It had to be 20 degrees below zero. By the time he had stepped out of his car to put the old man on the train the wind was so strong that his face was beet red. Kisliak got back to the old man's house late that afternoon. He stopped off at the house just to pick up a few things and make his way back to the camp. It was now about 7 o'clock at night and it was pitch dark as he came through the gate. The guard recognized him and gave him a snappy salute. He went immediately to the camp's hospital. Kisliak entered the hospital with great expectation and immediately saw Contessa Garcia, but there was no sign of Nina. He approached Contessa and with some difficulty, asked where Nina was. This drew suspicion from Contessa. "Why are you so interested in this girl?" she asked. "I'm here to help her escape. I know who you are," Kisliak whispered to her. Contessa drew back in alarm and only when Kisliak had fully explained his interest in Nina did Contessa finally step back and look at him, studying his facial expressions, trying to find a good reason to believe him. Contessa told him Nina would not remember him and Kisliak was taken back. "I thought you said she was well?" "Her body is healed but her mind has completely blocked out the past. When will you take my daughter?" she said with a fearful look. Kisliak tried to reassure her, "She will be safe with me because I love her. I will take care of her; there are no options here in the camp for her. I am her only hope, you must trust me." Contessa knew he was right.

Suddenly the door leading into the hospital room swung open and in came Nina. The major could not see any change in her. To him, she was still beautiful. When she stood by Contessa, he looked for some reaction from her but none was coming. Her reaction to Contessa was as if she had met her for the first time. This gave Kisliak a weird feeling inside him. This woman had been part of his life and he was not able to cope with this. Still he must remain focused on getting her out of the camp. He told Contessa he had his car outside. Kisliak asked Contessa to give her a sedative so she would not resist him when he tried to get her into the trunk.

Contessa's thoughts were moving at great speed. She would never see her daughter again. What if he couldn't be trusted? After going over it in her mind, she came to the conclusion that there was no choice. Nina would die in this camp if she did nothing. He was her only hope. Contessa told Nina that she must go with this man and do exactly what he told her to do. Nina seemed to be confused by what was going on. *Why are they taking me away from Contessa who she felt secure with? Who was this man?* Kisliak had to be careful with Nina because she seemed very fragile at this point and the wrong move could cause a setback in her condition.

In the middle of the night, Contessa and Kisliak lead Nina to Kisliak's car. He opened the trunk and gently helped her in, all the while assuring her of her safety. When the trunk had closed, Contessa, with one last show of emotion, laid across the trunk of the car and wept briefly for her lost baby. Kisliak gently moved Contessa away from the car. "Please," Contessa pleaded, "watch over my dear Nina, my baby." Kisliak reassured her he would always look after Nina, for he, too, loved her.

As he drove away, he looked in the back window and saw Contessa crouched over on the cold ground.

Kisliak had no trouble getting through the guards at the gate. They had seen him several times with the commandant. So, they assumed he was no security threat.

Kisliak drove about two miles when he stopped the car and let Nina out of the trunk. She sat next to him on the passenger side and they talked as they rode to the house. She seemed to be at ease with him. That night, the two sat near the old fireplace with the fire burning brightly. Kisliak was trying to jar Nina's memory of the past. He soon discovered that she had no recollections about her past at all.

Later that night, he gave Nina the bed and he slept on the chair until morning. After breakfast, which consisted of tea and stale bread, Kisliak and Nina set out to the railroad station. He must return to Moscow. His original plan was to leave Nina at the old man's house until the hunt for her would die out. Last night at the fireplace convinced him that she was not capable of being on her own, at least not just yet.

Before returning to his office, he drove Nina to his small dacha outside of Moscow. Sonia was still in their winter quarters in Moscow. There, he instructed Nina not to leave the house. He would return that evening after his duties for the day were completed. When Kisliak returned to his office, he was met by Colonel Zaitsev's secretary who informed him that the colonel had died of a heart attack the day before. The Center wanted him to call them immediately. After the original shock wore off, he called the center. His call was transferred to the Commanding General.

The Center had decided to have him take over the Colonel's duties. Kisliak would now be free to go back and forth to take care of Nina. There would be no one checking on his whereabouts since he was now head of the department.

The weeks went by quickly for Nina and Kisliak. They began living as man and wife. By now, they had become intimate and life for Kisliak became one happy day after the other. Nina had changed. She had become a very happy lady. Many times, he would hear her singing in the kitchen while she was making his supper. It would not be long now when the now Lt. Colonel Kisliak would retire and he would be able to spend more time with Nina.

The winter lasted longer than it normally should. The snow and ice were halfway up the door of the dacha and the wind would howl like a wolf at night. All this time he was able to hid his activities from his wife Sonia. He was constantly away on supposed business for the KGB. Sonia never questioned him. She had no idea that Kislaik was leading this double life with Nina in their summer dacha.

Nina was serving dinner when a loud pounding on the door occurred. Kisliak went immediately to the door and asked who it was but there was no reply. The howling wind didn't help very much so he unlocked the catch on the door.

As he pulled open the door, he was knocked to the floor. Kisliak looked up at a snow-covered figure that was unrecognizable. The figure held a gun in his hand, while Nina remained calm and looked unconcerned at the intruder. After the snow had fallen away from the intruder, a man in his thirties appeared.

Before the man could speak, Kisliak let out a low sorrowful cry. "Is that you Burke? I thought you were dead!"

"No thanks to you," the Irishman said. He gazed over at Nina and said, "My love, my love, it is me, Kevin." No answer came from her, just a staring look. Burke recognized at once that she was not herself. "What have you done to her?" he shouted at Kisliak.

"I have saved her life!" he shouted back. Burke walked over to Kisliak and pointed his pistol at his head. "You had your chance boy-o, now it is my turn. When you try to kill an Irishman, you better be sure you finish him off because we don't like people going around trying to kill us. We are funny that way. When you shot me and threw me over the embankment, you thought I was dead. But I decided not to accommodate you. So, I crawled up the embankment bleeding like a stuffed pig and made my way to the main road. There I flagged down a truck that bought me into town. The driver knew the doctor in this town and he patched me up without any questions."

Burke held his gun alongside Kisliak's temple and was slowing squeezing the trigger when Kisliak jumped up at him. He grabbed Burke's gun hand in a strong grip, pulling him down onto the floor. The two men rolled around the floor and they took turns at pinning each other on the ground. While they continued to struggle for the gun, two shots rang out. A loud thump on the ground caught their attention. What they saw stopped their struggling. Nina was lying on her back with her eyes staring up at the ceiling. During the struggle, a bullet from Burke's gun had penetrated her chest. The two men knelt beside her, sobbing. Kisliak face was covered with tears that had no end.

Kevin Burke stood up and walked to the door with the gun still in his hand. He turned and looked at Kisliak, who was holding Nina's hand. "I see now that you loved her too. She was too much woman for one man." He walked out into the blinding Russian snow and disappeared.

Chapter 14

When Burke left the dacha, Kisliak kept staring at Nina's limp body. He bent over her and kissed Nina softly on the lips. As he rose from the floor, he thought he saw her eyelids move. His first reaction was to assume that he was wishing this to happen. Kisliak again reached over Nina's limp body and watched carefully. He was looking for some signs of life. Seeing none, he rose from the floor and walked over to the table. As he was walking he heard a low moan. He turned quickly and threw himself down near Nina's body. She was alive but just. There was no time to lose. He put her coat on and bundled her up in a heavy blanket. He remembered that half a mile down the road was a retired Russian Army doctor. Cradling her in his arms, he ran out into the cold, snowy Russian night. He placed her in the car on the passenger seat. To his horror, the car refused to start. Kisliak started to shiver. In his panic to get her into the car, he had forgotten to put on his coat and he was only in his shirtsleeves. Praying and cursing, he tried to start the car. Nothing was happening. *It has to be the battery*, he thought. The cold night air had drained the battery. *Maybe it's something else.* So, he jumped out of the car and opened the hood, standing there in the freezing night air. He was looking for a reason why the car was not starting. There it was; one of the wires had been disconnected. His first thought was that Burke had disconnected it so that he couldn't follow him. Quickly he connected the wires and got back into the car.

He was shaking so bad that he could hardly steer the car in the blinding snow as he tried to maintain control on the ice-covered road. After a treacherous ride to the doctor's house, Kisliak got out and pounded on the doctor's door. To Kisliak, it seemed forever before the doctor opened the door. Kisliak started to tell the doctor about Nina in the car but fainted dead away in the doctor's arms.

When Kisliak finally came to, he was wrapped in warm blanket on a cot. He found himself looking into a blazing fire coming from a large fireplace. He called out, "Is there anyone here?" The door opened from a room at the other end of the house. A tall man entered with long gray hair and a large smile across his face. "Well I see you are doing alright."

"Where is she?" Kisliak cried out. "Is she still alive?" The Doctor smiled at him and said, "Yes, but time will tell. I removed a bullet from her chest. It had hit no vital organs. Her body temperature had dropped but that was due to the cold night air. I would think that this woman is in for a bout of pneumonia. I can tell you that she is not out of the woods yet. How in God's name," the doctor asked, "could you come out in a night like this in your shirt sleeves? It is obvious that you are not a young man and I am still not sure why you fainted."

Colonel Kisliak fell asleep and didn't wake up until the following night. He rose from his cot and saw the doctor with his back to him, placing more wood on the fire. The Doctor turned and smiled at him. "I see you are back in the world again." The doctor took a stethoscope from a table nearby and examined Kisliak's heart. After awhile, he smiled, "You are a strong man."

"How is the woman?" Kisliak asked. "Well, as I expected, she has pneumonia and she should be in a hospital. But to risk taking her out in this weather would be too dangerous. I will do the best I can for her here. There is no choice."

The days had gone by and her temperature rose to 104 degrees. The doctor kept rubbing her down with alcohol. Kisliak and the doctor took turns trying to bring down her fever. They sat by her bed in shifts 24 hours a day administering to her whatever little they could do. Nina's fever finally broke but Nina had not spoken one word. The doctor was concerned and asked questions of Kisliak. "Did she experience any form of trauma," the doctor asked?

During his stay with the doctor, Kisliak did not discuss with him any information about Nina. The doctor didn't ask or seem interested in their personal life. He was aware of Kisliak being with the KGB. They lived a half mile from each other, yet they had never met before. It didn't pay to know too much about your neighbor's business in that area.

One evening, Kisliak was sitting by her bedside and she opened her eyes wide. "Major Kisliak," she said. "Where am I?" Kisliak was taken back. She hadn't called him Major Kisliak since he convinced her to go to Ireland on a visit. Again she asked, "Where am I?" Kisliak knew immediately she had come out of her amnesia. She was Nina again. How would he ever tell her what had transpired during her loss of memory? He quietly told her to say nothing to the doctor about who they were. "The doctor is under the assumption that we are man and wife." Nina looked at him and laughed. This did not go down well with Kisliak. After a few more days, they thanked the doctor and left for Kisliak's dacha.

It took Kisliak one whole night to bring Nina up to date. She seemed shocked that they were living together as man and wife. Kisliak's happiness soon disappeared. Nina wanted to know about Kevin Burke. He explained to her that Burke had shot her during the struggle with him. "Does he think I am dead?" she asked. "Yes, I would think so," Kisliak told her. "I must get out of here," Nina said. "I am afraid not," Kisliak said. "By now, they are looking for you and if they find out about the role I have played in this, I will be shot."

Colonel Kisliak left that morning for work. Nina drove him to the railroad station. He had been missing for about a week. He had no way of contacting the office due to the weather and Nina's condition. There was no phone in his dacha. After arriving at his office, he made several calls to the Center; he was convinced he had covered his tracks with the high command. When he arrived home that night after his long day at the KGB office, Nina had made his supper and they sat and ate in silence. After dinner she gave him a cup of coffee and she sat down next to him and looked into his eyes. It wasn't a look of love, but of one who had a deep affection for him. "Boris," she said, which took him by surprise since she never called him that before, "I know now that you must love me dearly. There aren't many men who would take the chances you did to save my life. I do have affection for you but you know I do not love you. I will stay here with you till you need me no longer." This was a woman who killed on request from her superiors. This was a woman with a hardness about her that he had never encountered in all his military service, yet she had turned into a warm, sensitive woman that would give her young life to repay an old man for saving her life. Kisliak was tempted to turn her down but he honestly believed he could get her to love him.

Colonel Kisliak, in his position as the head man at the Illegal Directorate of the KGB, began his plans to issue the legal papers and identification cards for Nina to travel in Russia. It took him one month to give Nina the necessary documents to move freely around Russia. Kisliak attained a position for Nina with a Russian travel agency. The company assumed that Nina was his mistress. This would be handled discreetly because the owner of the agency owed a big favor to Kisliak.

Kisliak and Nina lived a fairly happy existence for nearly five years. They went to work together, went to dinner in the evening after work, and attended the latest plays and ballets. It wasn't love but before long, they became intimate again. Life for Kisliak was again beautiful. A wonderful surprise came to Nina and Boris, a bouncing baby girl, 6 lbs 8 oz. and they named her after her grandmother, Contessa Garcia. Like her mother and grandma, she was illegitimate. There seemed no end to Boris' happiness. He felt Nina had finally become happy with him. Still, Sonia hadn't gotten on to Kisliak's secret life. He was missing for months at a time. Sonia assumed his duties had changed due to his replacement of Colonel Zaitsev.

One evening, Nina and the baby waited at the railroad station for him. It was something they did every evening on his return from work. They waited until all the passengers had left the train but there was no sign of Kisliak. Nina and the baby went back to the dacha, assuming he was held at the office and would return the next day. Kisliak refused to put a phone in the dacha. There were no phones in the area. These dachas were for important individuals who wished only for privacy.

Nina became concerned when he didn't return home the second night. So after three days, she dressed the little girl warmly and took the morning train to Moscow. Nina couldn't go to Kisliak's office because she didn't know what was wrong, if anything. When Nina got off the train, she went directly to a phone booth and called Kisliak's office. She asked to speak to his secretary, a Lieutenant in the KGB. He told her Kisliak was not available. Kisliak had to report to the commanding officer at the Center. Nina was aware that the Lieutenant knew who she was and was always very respectful to her. So, she asked him if he knew when the Colonel would be back. Lieutenant asked her if she was Nina. Yes, she said. He told her that he would meet her in 20 minutes at the railroad station and he hung up.

Nina and the baby waited for him for about a half-hour when he arrived in a military car. Pulling up to her at the curb, the door opened and the young lieutenant told her to get in. He looked at her and said, "I have heard how beautiful you are. The colonel didn't do you justice." Then he bent over and put both his hands on his head, he was sobbing. "I loved this man and he is in deep trouble." Nina waited patiently for him to continue. "They have taken him to the notorious Lubyanka. They say that he is a traitor that has given secret information to our enemies." Nina was shaking. She knew what they would do to him in the Lubyanka prison.

After awhile, the lieutenant offered any assistance that he could provide for her. But she couldn't hear anything he said after he mentioned Lubyanka. The Lieutenant left her at the railroad station and she sat there for five hours waiting for the night train to take her parked car at the railroad station. There she would continue on to Kisliak's dacha. When she arrived at the dacha, she put her little girl to bed and sat by the open fireplace, pondering her next move.

They would be coming after her soon.

Her first reaction was how to get the baby out of Russia. She would have to find Kisliak's old comrade who had flown her to Gulag 8. What did Boris say his name was? She couldn't remember. She did, however, remember the drinking place where Boris had told her he met with his friend. Boris had told her that his friend had some crazy ways about him and that he had met him at Stalingrad. This man was a pilot and he landed in a ditch where Boris and his infantry company were about to attack a machine gun nest. After pulling the pilot out of the wrecked plane, Kisliak told him to lay still and rest while his company was preparing to knock out the German machine gun nest. She remembered how Kisliak laughed when he told her what this crazy pilot did. Kisliak and his company had advanced towards the machine gun nest and were ready to close in on it, when the machine gun went quiet. Approaching the machine gun nest, he looked in and there was this pilot sitting on top of the machine gun with three dead Germans around it. The damn fool had circled the nest and jumped in and killed the German crew. That in itself was an accomplishment but to do it with his right shoulder and arm broken, was the act of a man without fear. They had become good friends and when their paths would cross now and then, it would result in some big headaches the next day.

Nina knew exactly where that drinking place was and she remembered that the pilot was a frequent drinker there. She hoped that when she saw him, he would remember her. He would have the advantage on her since she was in a coma when he brought her to the camp. The next day, she bundled her little girl and herself and took Kisliak's .32 pistol and silencer with her, which she placed inside her fur coat. She had enough rubles to last for about three weeks. Boris always kept this amount in his bureau drawers. Nina stood outside the dacha and knew this would be the last time she would see it. There had been some happy days with Kisliak. She took just one glance out of the back of the car window as she drove away. She would call the Lieutenant in Boris's office to see if there was any more information on him.

Nina got off the train and walked over to the newsstand to check the papers so see if there was any news on Kisliak. She had gone through the whole paper and was about to dispose of it when something caught her eye at the very bottom of the last page. A small notice read, "Executed today at Lubyanka prison, Colonel Boris Kisliak for treason to the state." She looked for a place to sit down. A weakness came over her. *What a shame,* she thought. He was a good man and he had fought valiantly for his country. Nina walked around Moscow till evening. She was blessed with a very good child. The little girl was not a fusser or a crier. She was a very easy child to manage.

When it grew dark, she left for the drinking place. After finding the place, she entered and sat a table at the back. It didn't take long for the place to fill up. Nina sat there all night, while her little girl slept on her lap. It was very close to closing time and Nina was growing restless. She thought to herself, *When this place closes tonight, I will have no place to go. I can't go back to the dacha.* She was becoming desperate. The bartender was about to close the door, when the door flew open and a small stout fellow entered. She took one look at the visitor and she knew this was her man.

The bartender ordered him out. This was Nina's opportunity to approach him outside the bar. Nina explained to Leonov who she was but drunk or not, he remembered her. "I am sorry I don't know your name," Nina said. "It is Sergei Leonov at your service Madame. Kisliak was a dear friend to me and we had some good times together." Nina told him that the Kisliak was executed at Lubyanka prison. This seemed to sober Leonov up. "What do you want me to do?" he asked. Nina replied, "I need to get out of Russia."

"Where will you go?" Leonov asked her. "To Ireland," she said. Leonov thought for a moment. "I can get a hold of a private plane and fly you to Finland. There you will have to get on a commercial plane to Dublin. I will have to fly under the radar at a very low attitude. That is our only hope."

"Do you have enough money for the commercial flight to Ireland?" he asked her. She answered with a shake of her head, no. "When you get there, tell them you are a tourist and afterwards, claim Irish citizenship on the grounds that your father was Irish born. Since you are illegitimate yourself, I don't know how you can prove you are your father's daughter. You will have to solve this once you get there. I have some money and I will give it to you when we meet again. Do you have a place to stay?" he asked her. "No," Nina replied. "Then come with me," Leonov said. "I have a rental apartment outside of Moscow." Nina and the little girl got into his parked car and drove to his apartment.

It was small and cramped. There was only one bed. Nina was anticipating, from what she had heard about him, to have to fight off his advances. Yet, Leonov proved to be the perfect gentleman. He gave Nina and the little girl the bed and he slept in a chair. The next day, Leonov left her to make arrangements with a private plane company. He was gone all day and towards evening he returned. He informed her that she and the baby would leave at 3 am that morning. It would be better to fly at night. There was better cover. They slept for a few hours and left for the private airfield. They traveled about 40 miles to get there and they were airborne at 4:10 am.

Flying very low, Leonov managed to get out of Russia without any incident. He explained to her that during his air shows, he had discovered a deserted airstrip just inside the Finnish border. "We will just about get there and I will have to continue with you to Helsinki to put you on a commercial flight to Ireland. I have no alternative since I will have to get back to the plane with fuel. There are no facilities on this deserted airstrip for refueling."

They landed on the deserted airstrip in Finland without any incidents. It was daylight. Leonov, Nina and the little girl headed to the nearest village, which on the map seemed to be about three miles away. When they arrived at the village, they stopped into a small restaurant and had breakfast. It was a sleepy little village and the owner of the restaurant was the only one working there. It was still very early in the morning. Leonov made inquiries on where they could rent a car. There were no car rentals in the town but the owner offered to call a man who owned his own car and would be able to drive them to Helsinki. Leonov told him to go ahead and call him. Within an hour, an older man appeared with still an older car and offered to take them for 50 German marks because that was all the currency Leonov could offer him.

When they arrived in Helsinki, they rented a small room in a cheap hotel. Leonov left them and went to the airport and bought their tickets to Ireland. After giving Nina the tickets, he placed in her hand, 300 German marks. This should get you started for a few days when you arrive in Ireland. Leonov had kept the village driver while this was going on. He turned and said goodbye to Nina, who kissed him lightly on the side of his face, thanking him for what he had done. He then drove off with the hired driver.

Nina landed in Dublin and went straight to the hotel she had stayed in when she came to Dublin the last time. That was the time she was working undercover for the KGB. After taking the little girl around Dublin, she went back to the hotel and went straight to bed. They both slept till 8 am the next day. After breakfast, Nina and the little girl took a train down to Galway City.

Nina decided to talk to the authorities after she had settled down in Galway. She was going down to her father's house in Connemara. Three and half hours later she stepped off the train and rented a car to drive to Connemara. Something she thought she never would have done without the generosity of Leonov.

As Nina droved down to Connemara, she was tempted to stop at Nana Burke's house. She thought about it and decided to go by it.

When she got to Martin Connolly's home, she remembered how run down it was. It took her three days to straighten the inside of the house. The postman had arrived twice since she arrived there. She knew how quickly the news would get around that she was living there. The postman had informed Kevin Burke's mother that a young woman and child were settled in the house. From his description of Nina, Nana Burke recognized who Nina was. A few days later, Nana Burke had made some scones and set off for Martin's house. She walked the whole long stretch of road to his house. The Galway people are a hardy lot.

When Nana Burke got near the house, she saw a little girl sitting outside on the grass. With great expectations, she approached the child. She kept thinking that this could be her grandchild. *It must be Kevin's baby*, she thought. When Nina opened the door, Nana Burke threw her arms around her. "How glad I am to see you love," she said. Raving and hugging the little girl, she asked Nina, "Where is Kevin?" Nina was a little surprised. "After your blackout in your father's house, Kevin came back to me a very disturbed and depressed man. I haven't since him since. Tell me love," Nana Burke said, "is this my grandchild?" Nina was taken back. The Irish have a very direct way of speaking to you. They waste no time in getting to the point. "Oh I am afraid not, Mrs. Burke," Nina said. Nana Burke was stunned. "I thought you were both in love and you were planning to settle down."

"I am sorry," Nina said. "She is the daughter of a Russian colonel who is dead." Well, that is all Mrs. Burke had to hear. She was sizzling, and shoving the scones into Nina's hands, she turned her ass on Nina and said goodbye. Nina followed her out the opened door and shouted at her. "The Irish, I believe, have an expression, don't let the door hit your ass on the way out." She spent about 10 minutes cursing and damning Nana Burke.

In 1989, the Berlin wall was torn down and Martin Connolly, Nina's father, was united with her mother Contessa Garcia in West Berlin. Martin returned to Ireland after Contessa's death. When Martin reached his home in Connemara, he was a worn out old man. He had spent a lifetime waiting for Contessa. As he approached his house, he was surprised to see some activity around it. The house looked well kept and the grass was cut neatly. Maybe one of his sisters had come back.

Martin noticed for the first time a lovely little girl with dark hair playing in front of the house. Martin knelt down on one knee next to the little girl. Martin asked her, "What is your name, little one?" The little girl looked up into Martin's face. "My name is Contessa Garcia." She need not have answered that question. The moment that Martin looked at her, he knew. He put his arms gently around her little form. She snuggled up to him. "What are you crying for," the little girl asked him. "Oh Love, I am an old man and old men cry a lot." He looked up and saw Nina at the door and smiled. "Ah," he said, "you're the tricky one."

Nina helped him up on his feet and hugged him dearly. "My Dad, my Dad," she said. After a few minutes, they went into the house. Martin couldn't believe his eyes. What Nina had done to his house! It looked beautiful. "This was your work," he said. "Yes," Nina replied, "I thought it was my home and I should take care of it. It was alright for me to do that?" "Yes, yes," said Martin, "It is your home as long as you and the little girl want to live here."

It was late in the evening when Martin and Nina had exchanged what had transpired during the time he had seen her last in West Germany. Nina told him about Nana Burke and that she never returned again after her first and last visit. They both laughed.

Finally, Martin broke down and told Nina of her mother's death and of her mother's bravery and courage all through the terrible years in the Gulag camps. He told her about the night when she crossed the border, their meeting, and how she died in his arms that same night. Their time was so short that Contessa never got to tell him about his daughter.

Martin asked her if she was going to seek out this Kevin Burke fellow. She told him no, that it was better to leave matters the way they were. They discussed their financial situation and they came to the conclusion that Martin's pension from the German hotel he had retired from would cover their household expenses but they would need more money to continue to live properly on the farm in Connemara. They both agreed that Nina would go into Galway City for a job and Martin would take care of little Contessa. It wasn't very long before Nina was commuting back and forth from Connemara to Galway City. She obtained a position in an Irish bank in the foreign exchange department. Once again, Nina was happy living with Martin and the baby, although there were times she would contemplate on whether or not to look for Burke. She always pulled back.

One fine spring morning, she was at her desk in the Irish bank when she glanced over to see the line of customers facing the teller's cages. Nina had to look twice because she couldn't believe her eyes. There he was, Kevin Burke as large as life. She started to tremble and found that she had no control over her body. What was she to do? Kisliak told her that Burke had left that night from the dacha believing that she was dead. She reached out for an Irish expression. Nina thought that the Irish had the funniest expressions she had ever heard anywhere. What she was about to do would scare the living hell out of him. *By God, he deserved it,* she thought.

Leaving her desk, she smiled beautifully to the old Irish woman standing behind Burke on the line. The old woman motioned her to get in front of her. Gently, she leaned over Burke's shoulder and said softly in his ear, "There is an awful smell on this line. I think someone let go of a huge fart." Burke was deep in thought and this brought him out of it fast. Not turning around, he said in a very annoyed voice, "It would be well for you to hold your foul tongue woman." Nina's sides were bursting out of her trying to keep from laughing aloud. Then Burke's turn came to do his business with the teller. Nina looked over his shoulder to see what amount he was depositing. Burke was depositing a small amount of money. Nina spoke again over his shoulder, "By God for that sorrowful amount, you should be putting it into your piggy bank instead of taking up valuable banking time with that pittance."

Burke flew into a rage and turned around to tell this big mouth woman off. When he faced Nina, he turned white. He said, "I thought you were dead," and he sunk to the bank floor. As Nina looked at him on the floor on his knees, she thought, *What ever had happened to that hard rock of a man that nearly killed me in Nicaragua that night in the jungle?* She bent down and put her arms around him and helped him to his feet. Some of the bank customers were concerned and were asking her what was the matter with Burke. She looked up at the group and said, "Well you see he just looked at the interest he received from his account and it was too much for him to bear!" They all started to laugh and she brought him over to her desk.

While Burke was trying to recoup from the shock of seeing her, she never stopped laughing at him. Once again, Burke flew into a rage. "Listen woman, I never met a more aggravating SOB. I was doing fine when I thought I got rid of you."

"Well," Nina smiled, "you don't look the picture of happiness to me"

"Shut up woman, I think I am going to have a heart attack." Nina reached over and placed her hand on his arm, "I will be leaving soon, come home with me and I will give you a warm glass of milk and put you to bed, you old bastard."

Burke couldn't handle any more, got up from the desk and left the bank. When Nina left the bank that afternoon, Burke was waiting outside for her. He walked up to her, put his hands on her face and gently kissed her. They stood there in the middle of Galway City locked in each others arms for a long time.

Nina and Burke drove up to Martin's house, and little Contessa ran out to meet her. Burke was taken by surprise to see the little girl. During the ride home from Galway City, Nina never mentioned the little girl. He liked Martin Connolly the minute he met him. While Nina was preparing dinner, Burke was waiting for some explanation of this little girl he was looking at. After dinner, Burke cornered Nina in the kitchen and asked her about the child. She told him about Kisliak and herself. It didn't go down well with Burke. Shortly after that, he told Nina he was going home to his mother's house. He wanted to do some thinking about all that had happened. She offered him a ride but he said that he wanted to walk, that it might do him good. He also informed Nina that he had left the CIA and he had returned to Ireland to stay.

Nina waited a full week before she got a phone call from Burke at the bank. He sounded unsure of himself and she became uneasy at the end of the phone conversation. There was no commitment of another meeting. It was a cool ending. She didn't know this new Kevin Burke. He had changed from a strong and quite sure of himself man to the look of a broken man. A few months later, Martin Connolly joined his love, Contessa Garcia. He died of a heart attack one evening after dinner. Nina now was without anyone to take care of the little girl. How would she go back and forth to the bank every day, having to leave little Contessa alone? Nina, after some soul searching, left Connemara and rented a small cottage in back of a private house in Galway City. The Galway woman who owned the house and cottage took the little girl under her wing and she would look after little Contessa while Nina was working. This seemed to be working out very well for Nina.

Then one day at the bank a gentleman came in and sat down by her desk. He proceeded to ask questions about exchange rates. In the middle of the conversation, he stopped dead and proceeded to tell her that her friends in Moscow would like to talk to her. Nina's reaction was swift. "Get out before I call the Garda (police). I am finished with your lot and I am not going back to Russia." The man stood up and looked straight into her eyes, "That was a mistake," he said and he walked out of the bank.

That evening when the little girl had gone to bed, she sat alone and looked out her window. Her thoughts wandered back to the days with the KGB. It was so long ago; she found it hard to believe the things she had done. Nina knew that she had changed drastically. It was as though her past life had never existed. There was no way she was going to let the KGB bring her back to Russia. Nina knew she must be ever vigilant from now on.

Kevin Burke, now living with his mother, had become a very depressed man. He slept all day and went out every night to Galway City and drowned himself with Guinness. He was constantly in one fight after the other. One night he got in a fight with two country boys from outside the city. He was taken out of the pub and given a bad beating, leaving him busted up and bleeding on the street.

Nina was working late that evening and on her way home from the bank; she came across Burke on the ground. At first she didn't recognize him, but on a second look she knew it was Burke. She bent over and lifted his head up to her. He was a terrible mess, bleeding from his nose and mouth. She helped him to his feet. "Well, woman," he said, "what are you looking at?" Nina snapped back, "Not much." Nina helped him back to her cottage, where she cleaned him up and attended to his cuts. She put him into her own bed and that night she slept on the couch. The next morning was Saturday and the bank was closed.

While Nina was making breakfast, Burke was standing in the living room looking at the little girl. Burke finally sat on one of the chairs with the little girl opposite him. "Well," he said, "did the cat got your tongue?" The little girl started to laugh. "What are you laughing at," Burke said. The little girl placed her hand over her mouth, "You look funny". Burke was in no mood for small talk. He was hung-over from the night before and was aching from the beating he received from the two country boys. Nina came out of the kitchen with a plate of eggs and toast. Burke looked at the plate and growled, "Where the hell are the rashers?" Nina was also in no mood for any mouthing off from Burke. She hit him a belt across the back of his sore head. Burke was out of the chair in a split second and went for Nina. Nina let go with a frontal Karate kick to Burke's groin, laying him out on the floor. Nina stood there shaking her head, "You will never learn my Irish friend." The little girl started to cry. Nina went over to the little girl and cuddled her. She whispered into the little girl's ear, "Always aim for that spot honey. This will take the big macho out of them."

Nina took little Contessa into the garden and started to water the grass. It was not too long when Burke appeared in the garden. Nina, with the hose in hand, did not like the look of Burke as he came towards her. "Oh," Burke said as he moved closer to Nina, "I have something for you woman."

"Yes," said Nina, "and I have something for you," turning the hose full force in Burke's face. Burke had enough and he just sat down on the grass. He looked up at her and told her "she would have made a fine companion for the Marquis de Sade." Nina walked over to Burke and bent down and pushed him on his back on the grass, where she proceeded to kiss him. Nothing had changed. The kisses had the same magic that they had in St. Stephen's Green many years ago.

A year later with little Contessa as their flower girl, Nina and Kevin married in Galway city. The marriage was a bit stormy, especially when Nina lost her temper. It was not unusual to pass by the cottage to see Burke and Nina exchanging karate kicks. Still, they were very much in love. There were more moments of tenderness than when they lost their tempers and proceeded to exert the maximum damage on each other.

Kevin Burke was hired by the bank that Nina worked in. The couple moved back to Martin Connolly's house, which was now Nina's, and Nina stayed home with the little girl. Kevin went to work every morning to the Bank in Galway City. The Russian Intelligence had changed and Nina was no longer a priority for them.

Chapter 15

Sonia Kisliak sat opposite a gray-haired man in a small one-room apartment in a run down area outside Moscow. A small wooden table separated Sonia Kisliak from the gray-haired man. He sat in the only chair left in the room. The walls were peeling from years of neglect and the ceiling looked like it would fall down any minute. The one room was very damp and a very old heater was the only heat afforded them. The gray-haired man was Sergei Leonov. He had tracked down his old companion's wife, Sonia. She had lost her apartment in Moscow and her country dacha. After Colonel Kisliak was executed, all privileges were taken from her. She lost all the salary coming to her husband, which would also have included his pension rights. She was destitute.

Nina took all the rubles that the colonel and Sonia had saved when she fled from the Kisliak's dacha. Sergei had come to help his old comrade's wife. He never mentioned that he was the one that flew Nina out of Russia.

Sonia Kisliak was a woman in her late sixties. She looked much older. Sonia told Sergei that she suspected Colonel Kisliak of seeing another woman. Sonia remembered that from the time her husband met Nina in Colonel Zaisev's office, he couldn't stop talking about her. She thought that Nina was the one he was involved with. The KGB refused to answer any questions or give out details on her husband's execution. They only said he was a traitor and he would be executed. She was

129

allowed to see him before he died but that was only for a short visit and there were guards all over the room. Tears flowed from her eyes as she told Sergei that her husband told her that he was sorry for what was about to happen to her.

During her conversation with Sergei, she asked what had happened to Nina. He replied, "I heard a rumor that she was in Ireland but it was only a rumor." Sergei was not watching Sonia's eyes too closely or he would have seen the hate they held when Nina's name was mentioned. They talked about the good times he had with her husband. After tea which he noticed was all she had left in the closet, Sergei left, but not before he placed in Sonia's hands an envelope that contained enough rubles to keep her going for another six months. He had given everything he possessed in his savings to her. When Sergei had gone, Sonia had cried bitterly. As she walked passed the mirror that hung on the wall, she looked into it. "Nina Garcia, you will pay dearly for what you did to me."

The next morning Sonia called the young lieutenant that had been Kisliak's secretary. He was the same young man that had told Nina about the colonel being taken to Lubyanka and offered to help her anyway he could. Sonia had spoken to him many times when she would call her husband at the office. Sonia had invited him for dinner different times when he was working for Kisliak. The lieutenant was most anxious to help his deceased colonel's wife. They made arrangements to meet at a small park not far from the office. This meeting was a very dangerous one for the lieutenant. It was suicide for one's career to meet with the family of an executed traitor. Immediately Sonia came to the point. "Please, if you have any feeling for my husband, tell me where that slut Nina is located." The lieutenant turned pale. "I honestly don't know but I will try to find out for you."

The lieutenant went back to headquarters and started looking through the files of Colonel Zaitsev. He remembered that the colonel had a copy of Kisliak's orders to go to Ireland and bring back Nina. After some hours looking for the file, he located it. It indicated that Kisliak was to land in Dublin with a tour group. He then continued on to Galway himself, where Kisliak believed Nina was in her father's house in Connemara, Galway.

After receiving the information from the lieutenant, Sonia used the rubles that Leonov had given her to buy a ticket to Dublin. That following day, Sonia Kisliak met with a KGB agent in Dublin at one of the largest hotels. She was given his name by the young lieutenant who had been so sympathic to her loss. The agent informed her that a ex-KGB agent named Gregor Orlov was the one that had Kevin Burke under surveillance when he met Nina in Dublin. The agent was now retired and living in Ireland. Sonia got in touch with that agent and he related to her that Burke and Nina were married and living down in her father's house in Connemara, Galway. The last report he saw said that Nina was working in a bank in Galway city.

Nina and little Contessa had met Kevin Burke at the bank for lunch. The little one was off that day from school. She attended a school in Galway City. Every morning, Kevin Burke dropped little Contessa off at school as he drove into work. Nina and Burke were chatting on the bank floor and the little girl was standing outside the bank. When Nina said goodbye to Burke and started towards the bank door, she noticed an old woman talking to the little girl. The older woman was first to speak. "She is a lovely little girl." Nina laughed, "Well sometimes she can be a very lovely monster." They both laughed. Nina noticed that the woman spoke with a Russian accent. She had never met

Kisliak's wife, yet that was who she was. She continued the conversation with the older woman in Russian. The old woman told her she was looking for work and that she and her husband came to Ireland many years ago on a holiday and fell in love with the country. The old woman told Nina how she felt so at home in Ireland, she decided to leave Russia for good. Sonia informed Nina that she was waiting to hear from the Irish government on her request for asylum. Meanwhile she was sightseeing in Ireland. Nina felt sorry for the old woman and invited her back to the house for dinner. The feeling of speaking again in one's own language was uplifting to Nina.

They drove back to Connemara and they indulged in a strong steady conversation on what was happening in Russia. After dinner, Nina invited the old woman to stay over till the morning. She would drive her to Galway City in the morning to catch the train to Dublin because Burke had left that afternoon from the bank on a overnight business trip. They chatted into the night and only once did Nina notice a flash of hate in the old woman's eyes when she thought Nina wasn't looking directly at her. Nina passed it over as a wrong observation.

The old woman slept in Nina's bed in the same room with the little girl next to her. Nina slept on a couch in the living room. Nina was awakened in the middle of the night with a choking feeling. She stared up and found the old woman with one hand choking her and with the other hand she held a long knife. Nina grabbed the hand with the knife and started to tussle with the old woman. To her surprise the old woman was very strong. Nina found her own strength diminishing during the struggle. The old woman had bought a hunting knife in Dublin and brought it down with her to Galway. The two women had rolled along the floor and finally Nina disarmed her. "What the hell is the matter with you?" Nina shouted. The old woman was having a difficult time breathing. Nina sat her up on the couch and gave her a glass of water. She didn't look good. Nina tried again to find out why she had tried to kill her. At first the old woman said nothing but suddenly she grabbed Nina's hand and fell to the floor. She was having a heart attack. Nina listened to the gasping old woman who was whispering in her ear, "You were responsible for my husband's death." One more time, she reached up to grab Nina's throat. It was her last effort and she fell back, dead on the floor. Nina stood up and shook her head.

These Russians are tough babies.

Kevin Burke returned from his business trip that next evening. In good form, he started squeezing Nina in the kitchen while she was preparing dinner. "Tell me my love, what sort of day did you have?"

Nina replied, "How do the Irish say it? It was a grand day."

Printed in the United States
82983LV00002B/71/A